CHAPTER ONE

MONDAY DAY SHIFT BLUES

This old Factory has seen some changes over the years since it opened in 1978. Recently it was purchased by JJ and given to his Mum Terry. Before that a wee Irish guy named James Healy owned it. A Mr Longshanks tried to buy the Factory and turn it in to flats so the Irish Gentleman got in there first and saved it.

Before that in the early to mid-80's it was Fullerton Fabrications and that employed a lot of the local area and originally it was a Slaughterhouse for pigs but it got shut down. These days it's still a Textile's Factory and has been since 1987 and here's what the lassies of the Factory have been getting up to.

There's seven lassies on the day shift at the Textiles factory. Donna, Kirsty, Jan, Clare, Debbie, Lisa and Babs. The new owner of the factory, "Terry", is a lovely wee woman. She was given the factory by her son JJ and soon to be daughter in law Teresa. The lassies are due to clock in any minute now.

"My heid is burling Donna", said Debbie. I canny mind leaving Healy's yesterday after the karaoke".

"Ye were in some nick wummin. Me and Jan had to put you in a taxi. You only had a fiver on you so Jan gave the guy a flash of her tits to cover the rest of the fare. Here comes Jan noo".

"Morning ladies!!" said Jan. "Fuck me Debbie, you were in some nick yesterday were ye no hen?".

"Aye Jan".

"I can hardly be fucked with this shift today, wit a riot that was yesterday. Thank fuck Hugo had some decent Coke on him or I would've been in that taxi with ye".

Lisa and Babs come strolling in next.

"Morning Ladies!!"

"Morning!!"

"Did you see Kirsty on your travels girls? She's always fecking late" says Donna.

"Naw, never seen her ootside or that" says Lisa.

Clare wasn't with the girls yesterday because she plays football in her spare time. Jan doesn't miss her though when she comes in next.

"Where were you yesterday? Ye missed a cracking day in Healy's. Debbie spewed her ring in the bog and Kirsty was mad wi it as well. I was trying to fire into Alberto but he was having none of it".

"Och I was playing Fitba lassies, I scored four goals".

"Aw well done love" said Babs.

"Cheers Babs".

It's seven o'clock now and all the machines start rolling and there's still no sign of Kirsty. Terry walks up to the Production Line.

"Morning Ladies!!"

"Morning Terry!!"

"Girls, we have that big order for that company in Edinburgh to get out this week so I need you all to be on the ball to get it out for Friday. Ermmmm, where's Kirsty?"

"Eh, she's just nipped to the toilet" says Donna.

"Ah ok then" says Terry.

"So, as I was saying, we need to be on the ball this week to get this order out. I'll see you in Healy's at lunch time ladies".

"Where the fuck is she?" says Jan.

"Och Christ knows, ye know what she's like" says Donna.

Just at that, in strolls Kirsty. Late again.

"Och lassies I'm sorry. Has Terry been round yet?"

"Aye she has" says Debbie. "Donna said ye were in the toilet".

"Has any of ye's been in that Lassies toilet recently?" says Jan. "There's a right funky smell coming from it. I'll report it to Terry".

The lassies get cracking on with that big order for Edinburgh.

In Terry's new office, she has a picture of JJ on her desk, and a bunch of flowers from him and Teresa as well, for her new role. It wasn't long ago that she was on that production line with the lassies. Her PA "Bonnie" takes her in a cup of coffee.

"How's the new role going then Terry?" says Bonnie.

"Och to be honest, I'd rather be down there with the girls. I think once I've had this coffee, I'll head down and give them a hand with this big order. What did you get up to at the weekend Bonnie?"

"Och just the usual Terry. Me and my pal Marie who's recently divorced, went oot looking for men. She's been riding the best man from her wedding recently and he's got a one inch cock. Fuck driving two hours for that nonsense, she's embarrassing. I took her oot to Healy's to find her a real man but nobody will touch her because he's gave her the clap. I gave her some of my cream cause I've got hunners of it. I never seen you oot Terry".

"Och I've had too much on with this new role. I had Teresa round most of the weekend as well, picking out baby names and baby clothes and stuff. We all can't wait for the new arrival. It's their wedding as well a month before the baby is due so a lot is happening over the next few months".

"Do they know what they're having yet Terry?".

"No, they don't want to know either. As long as the baby is healthy then that's all that matters".

"Aye" says Bonnie.

The girls are cracking on with the work. Clare is going through all her goals step by step to Babs & Lisa. Jan is taking the piss out of Debbie spewing all over the toilets in Healy's. Donna and Kirsty are chatting away about a competition Kirsty won on her Social Media account. She's forever entering and winning them.

The phone goes off in Bonnie's office.

"Jan, that's the phone fur you", says Bonnie.

Jan heads up to the office.

"Jan, it's Hugo. Don't worry about that money for that gramme of Coke I gave you yesterday. Dae the nightshift need any more Gear?"

"Aye, they will do Hugo".

"Ok, I'll be over at the bookies from about 11, are you going to Healy's for lunch?".

"Aye, I'll be in there just after 12".

"Right, I'll get you in there. Right, catch ye later on".

"Nae bother Hugo".

Jan heads back down to the line.

"Who's phoning you at work Jan?" asks Donna.

"Och it was just Hugo".

"Are you riding him?" says Lisa.

"Um a fuck, I'd ride him like a Grand National winner though".

Its approaching midday and the lassies are getting ready for their lunch at Healy's. Since JJ and Teresa took it over, they provide the lassies from the factory with a free lunch as they're all part of the same family now. The lassies get paid by the Factory but spend most of their money in Healy's anyway. The 12 o'clock hooter goes and all the girls head to the bar.

"Are you coming for lunch Terry?" says Bonnie.

"Aye, I'll be over in five Bonnie".

Everybody leaves for lunch and Terry has a wee moment to herself. She looks out onto the shop floor that she once worked on and just takes a wee look round the empty factory. This is all now hers. She takes in a deep breath and locks the front door. Time to visit her son and future daughter in law in their new bar now. A lot of good things have happened in this small town recently. That though, is about to change.

CHAPTER TWO

HEALY'S

Healy's was rocked recently by the resignation of Mel, she decided to go backpacking around the world on a whim. She just left one day and didn't even tell anybody barring sending a letter that was full of spelling mistakes which suggests she was in a rush to go.

Tina from the bookies has taken over the bar and her no nonsense approach in the bookies is why JJ wanted her to take over from Mel and run Healy's.

Sandra got hired as well much to the dismay of her man Colin as there's not another decent bar in the toon and she can keep an eye on him noo.

There's a photo behind the bar of auld Sadie. She was an auld woman that worked in here in the 1990's and died in the pub. She's still very much missed in this town and JJ and Teresa named the wee snug in the bar after her.

JJ had a lot of explaining to do to Teresa after he proposed to her, especially about the lucky Bunnet, but they've settled into their wee lives here now and the pub is doing well.

The factory girls are all sat in "Sadie's snug" eating their lunch. They're all eating except from Debbie.

Jan is still ripping the pish out of her and Debbie just keeps looking at the toilet door with her hands on head. That's where all of her food and alcohol ended up yesterday as it all came out of her mouth and covered the place. She can't face any food today and is on her fourth pint of water.

Hugo walks into Healy's and immediately starts looking around.

"Tina, you seen Jan aboot pal?" Aye Hugo, she's in Sadie's snug wi the rest of the Factory Girls".

"Cheers pal".

Hugo heads over to the snug. "Jan, come oor here the noo".

"Fuck sake Hugo, I'm hawf way through my steak pie here".

"You'll no be able to eat it in a minute if you don't move yer arse".

Jan and Hugo head over to the quiet bit of the pub where the jukebox is.

"Right Jan there's 20 grammes of Gear in that envelope for the nightshift. Just give me the money when they square you up as usual and I'll give you another gramme of Coke ok. Aye nae bother Hugo".

Hugo heads over to Colin, John and Tony who are in for their usual lunch time two pints.

"How's it going lads?"

"Aye no bad Hugo" say the lads.

"Put a pint on the tap for the boys Tina and I'll have an Orange Juice and get yourself one hen".

Hugo pulls out a crisp £50 note, that's all he ever has. Tina pours him his drink and gives him his change.

"What was Hugo wanting Jan?" asks Donna. "Och he was just giving me the Gear for the nightshift. Do you want a gramme?".

"Dae a fuck Jan. Never touched the stuff and never will" says Donna.

"Och just get to the toilet and fire one doon ye wummin".

"Fuck that!! You better watch Terry doesn't catch you ya maddy, you know she hates drugs".

"Och, she'll no find oot if yous aw keep yer mooths shut".

Terry walks into the pub and heads over to the snug.   "Have you seen oor JJ lassies?"

"Naw" says Lisa, "he must be in the office". Terry heads through the back to the office. "JJ, Teresa, how are my two favourite people?".

"Aw hiya Maw, how are you darling?"

"Busy darling, we've got a big order in for a company in Edinburgh so we're dealing with that son".

"How are you Teresa?"

"Och my back is killing sure but these accounts won't do themselves".

"JJ, hire an Accountant and let Teresa put her feet up for these last couple of months".

 "I told her that Maw, but she won't fecking listen to me."

"Language JJ" says Teresa.

"Sorry baby".

The bar door opens and in walks Donald with his brother. He spots Hugo and walks to the other side of the bar. Tony spots this and decides to stir the pot.

"Donald, dae we fucking smell or summin ya cunt? No no Tony, just want a quiet pint with my brother thank you. What did you do to him Hugo?" asks John. "Och absolutely nothing boys. He still blames me for some Moroccan bird leaving him twenty odd years ago which isn't true. The cunt won't just wipe his mouth and move on. Fuck him!!"

The bar door opens again and in walks Marie. She makes a bee line for Bonnie and asks to speak to her. Bonnie and Marie head over to the jukebox area. "Bonnie, that cream isn't working, my fanny is still on fire with the itchy and scratchy show". "Well it's your own fault ya dafty, you knew what he was like but never listened to anybody, it's your own fault".

The boys are all looking over at her in disgust.

"Dirty fucking midden" says Colin. "She had a great guy and ended up with not only a fandan but the best man from her wedding".

"The lowest of the low" says Tony. "What happened to her ex man anyway?" says John.

"He went to Spain" said Hugo. "I still have a few contacts over there, he was a good pal of mine so I sorted him out with some work, he's doing well over there".

"Good", said John. "I hope he gets a hold of his so called best man one day and punches him right out of his trainers".

"He doesn't give a fuck" says Hugo. "He finds it all hilarious, he knows how much of a dirty bastard his ex pal was so now he knows she's riddled. He's having the time of his life over there and he's due back soon for a visit".

"Are you going to eat something Debbie?" said Babs. "Babs I honestly couldn't, I don't feel right at all". "Stop being a fanny" says Lisa.

"You want me to ask Alberto to make you a fried egg sandwich"? asks Jan.

Debbie gets up and runs to the toilet hawding her mooth. All the lassies burst oot laughing.

"You're a bitch Jan" says Clare.

"Och I know hen".

Terry's mobile phone goes off in JJ's office.

"Who's that Maw?".

"I'm not sure son, some foreign number".

"Answer it then!!"

"Hello? Yes speaking. How many units? Yes we can manage that. Yes, hold on until I get a bit of paper".

Teresa gets Terry a bit of paper and a pen.

"003 505 401 7604"

"What did you say your name was again? Ok, Edu, I'll be in touch with a price".

"Who was that maw?"

"Some guy from a company in Gibraltar, wherever that is, wanting a quote for a job. JJ, we haven't had a job this size before, it's ten times the size of anything we've ever had".

"Aw I'm made up for you maw, well get on it then".

"I will son, I will".

Debbie comes back from the toilet.

"There's a bit of a funny smell coming from that toilet too".

"Aye probably your dry boak fae yesterday" said Jan.

CHAPTER THREE   **WHO'S THAT GUY?**

The lassies get the Edinburgh order done and before they head to lunch on the Friday, Terry tells them all that there's going to be a big meeting after lunch. The lassies head over to Healy's.

"Wit dae ye think it's aboot lassies?" asks Donna.

"Well hopefully we're not gonna lose our jobs" says Debbie.

"Don't be so fucking stupid, there's plenty wee regular contracts that we still have so everything will be fine" says Jan.

"Well it canny be a wage rise because we just got one when Terry took it over" says Kirsty.

"She's probably gonna ask why the night shift are always fleeing on their shift haha" said Clare.

Jan's face is a picture.

"Och it canny be bad news because I'm sure Terry or Bonnie would've said. Yes, we're all work colleagues but we're all pals too" says Babs.

"I'm with Babs, it definitely won't be bad news" says Lisa.

Terry walks into the snug and it all goes silent.

"Lassies, it's not bad news after lunch so don't worry, it's just pretty important that's all".

"Phew" says Debbie.

The bar does open and this guy walks in with a smart suit on, nice shoes and a tan. He wheels in a big Green suitcase behind him. He looks completely out of place and walks straight up to Tina behind the bar and gives her a kiss and a cuddle.

"Who's that guy?" says Jan.

Nobody knows, all the girls are bewildered.

The guy orders a drink and Tina sits the pint in front of him.

Hugo walks in and goes straight up to the guy and gives him a massive hug.

Jan canny eat her Steak Pie for staring at the guy.

"Gie it a by you Jan" says Donna.

"Och nae wunner, look at him. Oaft!!"

"Simon, it's great to see you mate" says Hugo. "How's Spain man?"

"Och amazing pal, thank you so much for putting me in contact with Bruno over there. What a great guy he is!!"

"Och it's no problem at all pal. How long are you here for"?

"Just a few days mate, got a couple of things to take care of here Hugo".

"Anything I can help you with mate?"

"Na, I got this partner".

"Hugo, you no gonna introduce me to your pal?" says Jan.

"Fuck sake Jan, give the guy a chance to get a sip of his pint".

"Jan, this is my mate Simon".

"Jan, pleased to meet you pal".

"Likewise Si".

"She's a fucking riddy man" says Clare.

"He's got a cheeky smile" says Lisa.

It's time to head back to the Factory for the big meeting. Lunch time is over and the lassies are all nervous.

"So who was that guy then Jan?" asks Kirsty.

"You'll no fucking believe it lassies!! It's Tina from behind the bar's boy Simon. Apparently he moved away from the toon over 20 years ago, joined the Army & married that skank Marie, she left him and he moved to Spain. She came back here and he moved over there".

"I thought I recognised him" said Donna. "The tan threw me off and probably the 20 years since I last saw him".

"Ah, it all makes sense now" said Kirsty. "I wondered why he knew Tina".

Kirsty then gets her mobile phone out and starts texting.

"Put yer phone away Kirsty, Terry is about to come out for this meeting" says Donna.

"I'm entering that competition on the Radio, the answer is Wet Wet Wet, I know it".

"Ladies, I was going to let yous go early today at lunch time as a thank you for all your hard work on the Edinburgh contract but I have some news for yous. Big news!! We've had contact from a company in Gibraltar about a job. It's ten times bigger than any Contract we've ever had so I've given them a price and they've accepted it".

"Where's Gibraltar"? asks Lisa.

"Lisa, it's stuck to the bottom of Spain" says Bonnie.

"Ah, I see".

"So, go and enjoy your weekend as the hard work starts on this contract on Monday ladies" says Terry.

"Fuck it ladies, back to Healy's" says Jan.

"Aye, fuck it" says Donna.

"Hing on, hing on lassies" says Kirsty. "They're about to announce the winner of the competition on the radio".

"Welcome back to Radio Westside" says the DJ. "The answer to the question, which band was Marti Pellow the lead singer of was of course, Wet Wet Wet". "Congratulations to Kirsty at the Factory who's our winner of a £20 gift voucher at Sammy's Store. Congratulations Kirsty!!"

"You're a jammy bitch!!" says Donna.

"I know!!" says Kirsty.

The DJ comes back on the Radio.

"We have to interupt "Love Is All Around" for a special News Bulletin just in to us by the local Police".

"A female body has washed up on the shore and Police are asking for people to check on their relatives to see if any of them are missing".

"Detective Moriarty is on the line".

"Detective Moriarty, what do we know so far?"

"We don't know much right now other than the Woman looks between 40-50 and has the letter "M" tattooed on her neck".

"Fuuuuuuuuuuuck!!" Screams Bonnie. "That's Marie!!"

CHAPTER FOUR   MURDER IN THE TOON

There's been plenty of death in this toon over the years. Some folk know this toon as God's waiting room. But a Murder? That just doesn't happen here. The town is in shock but did she deserve it? The Murder is the talk of Healy's.

"Fucking deserved it the cow" says Tony.

"Aw come on man" says Sandra from behind the bar.

"Well she did, another Hoor less on the planet I say" says Tony.

"I'm with Tony" says Donald. "I mean, going with the best man from your wedding when she was still married to Simon, that's lower than a snakes belly that".

"Aye mibee, but they were separated but she didn't deserve what happened to her fur fuck sake", says Sandra".

"Doesn't matter if they we separated or no, he's a snakey bastard for even messaging Simon's wife and she's a slag for falling for it. They both deserve their Karma".

Bonnie walks in with the lassies and they change the subject.

"Can I get yous a drink Ladies?" says Sandra.

"Aye, just the usual for all of us darling" says Babs.

Sandra starts pouring all the drinks out and the lassies take their normal seats in the Snug.

"I just canny believe it" says Bonnie. "It's a bit of a coincidence that her ex man arrives in the Toon and she's found dead the same day eh?".

"I know, and I was talking to him at the bar as well" said Jan.

"Ladies, I wouldn't speculate just now, it might just be a coincedance" says Lisa.

"I know Simon from years ago, pretty sure it wouldn't be him" says Donna.

Sandra brings the drinks over and it's the talk of the place. The local news comes on the telly and it's the main news story. Reporters are swarming all over the town. They've been coming into the pub and Sandra has just chased them out. She's even put a sign on the door at the request of JJ.

"No reporters are allowed in the Bar to question the Patrons about the recent murder by order of the owners. You **WILL** be asked to leave the premises!!".

The whole pub is gripped by the whole thing and every time it comes on the telly, Sandra turns it up.

Reporter:- "We're outside the local Police Station with Detective Moriarty, is there anything else you can tell us tonight Detective?"

"Yes, we've made an arrest this evening to help us with our enquiries and that's all I can tell you at the moment. I'd urge the locals not to speculate at the minute and if they have any information for us regarding this matter no matter how small, then please let us know".

Reporter:- "Thank you Detective".

"Oh, I wonder who they've arrested lassies?" says Clare.

"Probably some junkie bastard" says Lisa.

"Aye, you know what they're like round here the black bastards" says Donna.

Hugo walks into the bar with Tina and her face is chalk white.

"Everything ok Tina"? asks Kirsty.

"They've arrested oor Simon. He never did it, he came straight here from the airport and has been with me and Hugo the whole time. The Polis don't believe his alibi at the minute because of Hugo's past but it's the truth. He hasn't left any of our sides since he's been back. They're checking the DNA found on her body and then he should be out hopefully".

"Fuck sake Tina, I was telling the lassies it wouldn't be him" says Donna.

"He honestly hasn't left mine or Hugo's side. He came from the airport straight here. Phoenix Taxi's all have trackers on their Taxi's so the Police are checking his Taxi now. He came straight here and then came to mines after my shift here with Hugo and then the Polis turned up".

"Any idea what happened to her Tina"? asks Bonnie.

"Yes Bonnie, she got stabbed in the neck twice and her throat was slit and they think she was dumped in the Harbour".

"My God Tina" says Bonnie.

"The Families Officer told me when she came to the house to tell us the news. Even though she did what she did to my son, none of us wanted this. Hopefully the Police get to the bottom of it soon. He or she could still be amongst us tonight".

"Scary biscuits man!!" said Clare.

Tina finishes her glass of Wine and Hugo drives her round the road.

"Things like this just don't happen round here girls" said Babs.

"Who would've had such a gripe with her to do this?" says Lisa.

"Fuck knows girls, I'm honestly racking my brains but I'm running a blank. The only person I can think of is her ex husband but you just heard his Mum" says Bonnie.

"She's obviously going to back her son up no matter what" says Donna, but Tina calls a spade a spade and she seemed pretty adamant that he hasn't been out of her sight and she woudn't lie about something like that. No way!!"

Once the drink starts flowing, folk start to forget about all the drama that's happened today. The lassies are having a ball in the snug and all the men are at the bar arguing about the Fitba. The wee town won't be the same until the killer is caught, but for now, the locals only have a hangover to worry about in the morning.

CHAPTER FIVE

WHO DUNNIT?

Tina opens up the bar and the first two people through the door are JJ & Teresa.

"Tina, you go home today, you must be worried sick. Don't worry, I'll run the bar until Sandra gets in later" says JJ.

"JJ, I'm fine son honestly. Detective Moriarty phoned me this morning. The Pheonix Taxi tracker came back and he came from Prestwick Airport straight to the Pub as he said he did. They've checked the airport CCTV as well and he got off his flight and straight into the Taxi as well".

"Well that's good news, he's ex Army so they'll know that he's pretty more than capable of this".

"JJ"!! says Teresa.

"You know what I mean Teresa. Those guys are trained to kill, I'm not saying he did it but you know what I meant eh Tina?".

"Aye JJ, I know what you mean. He is trained to kill obviously but he's very controlled and he's moved on massively with the situation involving Marie. He doesn't hold grudges, he just moves on and blocks the individuals out of his life. He's very ruthless with people that way".

"He once told me as well that wishes that Marie had a lifetime of happiness ahead of her and he meant it. He said that everyone deserves happiness, even her and that he just wasn't the one for her and that he was ok with that. Life goes on Mum he said".

"It's all very odd eh Tina?" says Teresa.

"It certainly is, I just know it wasn't him".

"Fair enough Tina", says Teresa.

The pub door opens and in walks Detective Moriarty with a young colleague.

"JJ, can I talk to you somewhere private please"?

"Sure, come into my office".

JJ and Teresa take the Detective and his colleague into their office and point to the two spare seats in the office and the Detectives sit down.

"What can I do for you Detectives?".

"I'm going to need the CCTV from the pub yesterday JJ. I'm sure you're aware of what's going on as Tina works here so I won't insult your intellegence. We're trying to piece together Simon's movements from when he arrived in the Country yesterday".

"No bother, I'll give you a pen drive now of yesterday's CCTV".

The Detectives take the pen drive and leave the premises.

The pub starts to fill up with all the regulars. The Fitba and the Horse Racing dominate the TV today. JJ speaks to Tina and tells her not to put the news on today so the town can try and get back to some sort of normality and let the Police do their job. Tina agrees.

Donald and his brother keep going between the bookies and the pub. Tony is ripping the pish out the both of them as they canny buy a winner between them. Alberto is keeping an eye on proceedings from his kitchen and decides to pop into the bar to add fuel to the fire.

"Yer brother's tips no working the day Donald?"

"Fuck you Alberto" says Donald.

The wee Italian heads back into his kitchen giggling away.

Colin & John always do a Fitba coupon together and they're waiting on Ayr United for £180 each.

"Let's go to Somerset Park and talk to our reporter JP Catania!!".

Reporter:- "It's bad news I'm afraid if you're an Ayr Utd fan. They've just conceded a 95th minute equaliser here".

"Baaaaaaaaaaaaaaaaaastard!!" shouts Colin.

"Cunts man" says John.

"Unlucky boys" says Donald.

"Feck off ya dick" says Colin.

The Karaoke is in full swing and the Factory Girls are hogging the mic as usual. Everybody is having an amazing wee night when somebody walks into the bar that nobody expected to see. Simon walks in followed by Hugo and then by Tina. Tina walks right up to the karaoke guy Jimmy and takes the mic off him.

The pub is packed with all the locals and everybody is braced for Tina's tongue. She doesn't mix her words so the pub is waiting with baited breath for her speech.

"Ok folks, listen in. As most of you know, my son here Simon was arrested and questioned for the murder of his ex wife Marie. They've checked every single bit of CCTV, Taxi Tracking devices, DNA and after a Post Mortem, Simon wasn't even in the Country at her time of death".

"His DNA isn't anywhere on her body at all but somebody else's is. I'm doing this tonight to save all the gossipmongers around the town having his name on their tongue any more. If anybody has anything to say about my son then please come and see him or myself and we'll gladly educate you. He's been proven completely innocent by the Police and he's a free man. Tina puts the mic down and there's a big cheer from the Factory Girls".

"Oan yersell Tina!!" shouts Jan.

"Fucking tell them" shouts Lisa.

Folk are shaking Simon's hand and patting him on the back. Hugo places a pint in his hand.

"You deserve that tonight pal".

"Cheers Hugo. It's been a brutal 24 hours in that Police station going through everything. I hope what I've told them can help them with their enquiries".

Jan, Kirsty and Donna have had a few now and decide that they're now part of the Flying Squad.

"Right, I knew it wiznae that handsome bastard" says Jan.

"Piss off Jan, you had him hung drawn and quartered earlier on" says Donna.

"I think it was that Donald, I don't like that creepy bastard. He's always looking over here at us the pervy auld cunt" says Kirsty.

"Alberto has got hunners of knives in there, might be him" says Donna.

"It'll no be that sexy wee Italian" says Jan.

"Do you fucking fancy everybody Jan?" says Donna.

"Keeping my options open Donna".

"It might be Hugo, Simon is his pal and we all know his history lassies. Maybe a wee welcoming home present for his pal" says Kirsty.

"Listen lassies, ye heard Tina earlier" said Donna. "The guy wouldn't want this to happen, he just moves on with his life. There's somebody out there that's done this, maybe even in this pub tonight watching one of us".

"Well fuck me sideways. I didn't think of that until now. I wonder who dunnit?" says Jan.

CHAPTER SIX

THE GIBRALTAR ORDER

It's been a bit of a mental weekend for the lassies. Clare got Player of the Tournament over the weekend at a wee Fitba Tournament in Glasgow and she's showing everybody her trophy. It's Babs and Lisa's turn to be dying this Monday morning. Jan spiked their drinks with some extra Vodka she had in her bag in the pub without them noticing.

"Right Ladies, this Gibraltar order" says Terry. "It's going to take us about a month to do it over the day shift and the night shift. I don't care if you're dying from the weekend, it's self inflicted. Get tore right in about this today ok".

All the lassies nod and the machines get fired up.

"Fuck me Babs, I'm absolutely dying the day" says Lisa.

"Me too honey, those Vodka's were a bit strong that Sandra was pouring eh?" says Babs.

"The ones Sandra were pouring weren't, but the ones Jan were, was".

"Jan"!! says Lisa.

"Wit? We were aw steaming and yous two were just sat there chilling oot in the corner having a blether so I helped yous along".

Bonnie and Terry are in the office when the phone goes. Bonnie picks it up.

"Hello, Bonnie speaking, how can I help you today? Yes, I'll just get her for you Sir".

"Terry, it's a guy called Edu on the phone for you".

"Edu!! How are you?".

Terry is on the phone for the next 15 minutes and she has a bit of an apprehensive look on her face when she comes off the phone.

"What's the matter Terry?" asks Bonnie.

"Edu is the guy who wants this Gibraltar order done. He wants a couple of his guys to come over for a couple of weeks and watch how we work and see the progress of the order for themselves". "I told him we don't normally do that but as it's such a big order then why not. They paid for it up front and he seems a decent enough guy so they'll arrive in a few days".

"Cool, I've no been with a Spanish guy before" says Bonnie.

"He's not Spanish Bonnie, he's Gibraltarian. You mibee wanna research some history before you come away with any of that nonsense in front of these guys".

Terry goes down and tells the lassies about their impending visitors to the factory and Jan is over the moon.

"I've no been with a Spanish guy before lassies!!".

Terry just rolls her eyes.

The new visitors coming is the talk of the snug in the pub at lunch time.

"I bet that Edu's pals are big Latino Love Gods" says Jan.

"Will you give it a rest Jan? You're like a walking hormone" says Debbie.

"There's no much talent aboot here so these visitors might be my only hope".

"Naw Jan, ye want to pump everybody aboot here. Maybe that's why" says Kirsty.

Aw the lassies burst oot laughing.

"These are my tits Kirsty and you're getting on them" says Jan.

"We've never had customers visiting the Factory before so I think it's a good thing" says Babs.

"I agree" says Lisa. "It would be good if we got a Celeb to visit wan day eh lassies?".

"Aye like Danny Dyer or something?" says Clare.

"Away and bite my shite. I canny stand that bastard" says Donna.

"How no"? says Debbie.

"His voice goes right through me and I've got mare talent in my little toe than he has in his whole body" says Donna.

"I think he's quite good looking" says Jan.

Terry is talking to JJ and Teresa at the end of the bar about the impending visitors that are coming to the Factory soon when Hugo overhears their conversation.

"Did you just mention Gibraltar there Terry?".

"Yes Hugo, we're doing an order for a company there".

"Ah really? I know the area well".

"Do you Hugo?".

"Yes, I lived there for a wee while back in the 1990's".

"So you did aye, I totally forgot all about that. I remember you gave JJ money the day before you were going on the Main Street there. Do you not remember that JJ?".

"No Maw".

"You used to stop poor Hugo here every single time he walked down Main Street for a pound. You must owe the poor guy thousands".

"What's the name of the Company Terry, I might know them?".

"I can't disclose customers details Hugo sorry pal".

"Ah that's fair enough then Terry".

"I'm sure you'll see them about soon Hugo. They're coming over to visit for two weeks in a few days time".

"Oh, they might have heard of me Terry".

Hugo walks over to Donald for chat.

"Right, I know we don't really get on these days but I'm just giving you a heads up ok. The factory is getting visitors from Gibraltar in the next few days for a two week visit. Keep your mouth shut about us staying over there ok?".

"Aye whatever Hugo, it wasn't exactly the highlight of my life being forced over there with you".

"You weren't forced ya bampot, just keep schtum right?".

"Aye, nae bother".

There's a wee bit of excitement building in the town for the impending foreign visitors. Business is good in the pub and the Factory. Let's see what the next few days brings.

CHAPTER SEVEN

BRINGING BACK OLD MEMORIES

Gibraltar being brought back up over the past couple of days has put Hugo on edge. It's Simon's last day in the town so Hugo asks to meet him in the pub at 1pm, not only say goodbye but to chat about old times.

Simon arrives about half an hour early to chat to his Mum behind the bar first.

"I'm sorry I didn't get to spend much time with you over the past few days Mum with all that's went on".

"Och don't be silly son. I still think you should stay a day extra and go to her funeral at least. She was your wife son".

"You've just said it Mum. She was, I'm afraid all of her decisions were her's, I'm just moving on with my life. The fact they haven't caught who done that to her yet would make it a bit awkward if I turned up. The only person arrested for it, and probably the guilty one too in her families eyes still".

"Aye son, I suppose you're right. You get back to Spain and enjoy your life. It's far too short".

Hugo walks into the bar.

"Si, Tina, how are we?".

"Aye magic Hugo, Orange Juice ma man?".

"Yuuuuuuuup".

"Away and sit doon you two and I'll bring yer drinks over" says Tina.

The bar starts to fill up with the regulars so Hugo and Simon head into the "Snug" for a bit of peace and quiet.

"Wit time's yer flight the morra mate?" says Hugo.

"0730hrs from Prestwick to Malaga pal. I wish I hadn't bothered my arse coming hame do you know that? It's been more hassle than it's worth. I didn't get anything done that I needed to do. I might need to pop back in about a month or so".

"Do you need a lift?".

"No no, I've booked Phoenix Taxi's in Irvine to come for me. Russell that owns it is a pal and his firm are always on the ball".

"Spot on Si".

"So, why have you been so uptight the past few days Hugo? It's no like you man".

"Och the factory are getting some visitors over from Gibraltar and it just brought back a load of memories for me Simon. "Good and bad pal".

"Like what?".

"Well, let's just say, that's where I made my money as I'm sure Bruno has told you?".

"Bruno hasn't told me anything pal. He's fiercely loyal to you and won't have a bad word said about you. You're still a legend over there Hugo".

"Well that's nice to know but unfortunately I can't ever go back there. Did I ever tell you about Siham?".

"Siham?" says Simon.

"Yes Siham. See this Orange juice Si? She's the reason I'm drinking that with you today and not a pint of lager like you. I met her over there pal and she was truly the love of my life. She died on a trip to Morrocco when she choked on her vomit after being out drinking. I vowed never to touch a drop of alcohol after that day and I haven't".

"Shit man, I never knew about that pal, I'm sorry to hear that".

"Well, it's only Donald that knows about it really as he was with me when it happened. It was a long time ago in the 1990's but to this day, I haven't even looked at another woman either".

"Hugo, I'm going to give you some advice mate, now please don't take it the wrong way either. I'm your real pal, not one of these folk round here that take your drinks off you and don't return them just because you're rich. I get you one back, not just because I'm your pal but because it's the right thing to do. You might not like some of what I'm about to say but pin your ears back for a change".

"Oh, ok Si".

"Siham has gone pal. Cherish her memory and remember the good times and they'll help you through the bad times, trust me. I get that you loved her and probably want to hold on to that and you should, but there comes a time when you need to accept that she's gone and move on with your life Hugo".

"Och I know you're right Si but it's difficult. I've been on my own that long now that I just accept it".

"Take me for example Hugo, I was with Marie for 16 years and when she ended it, I knew she meant it so didn't bother even trying with her, I knew there was no point. She had a mental breakdown the year before and was a shell of her former self. Hence all the rash decisions in life she made afterwards".

"I thought I would never meet anyone ever again too. Who'd want me I thought? When I moved out to Spain, I met a Jazz singer who just blew me away. I wanted her but I never told her because like you after Siham, I just wasn't ready and that wouldn't have been fair on her. She was everything that I ever wanted in a woman.

"Eventually we got together after about a year of dating other people. It didn't work out and I was devastated. Still to this day I don't know why she walked away from something perfect that we had, but you know what? My relationship with Marie taught me that life is too short pal. Don't dwell on it because it's not meant to be. What's meant for us has already been written out for us Hugo".

"Do you know what Si, you're spot on there pal. I do miss the feel of a wummin if I'm honest. Maybe it's time that I started to get among it again. Who'd want an old fart like me though?".

"That's what I'm saying to you. We all feel like that after a split when in truth, people have had an eye on us all along. Just look for the signs and go with it Hugo".

"I will Si, cheers mate. Oh, did the Polis give you your passport back then aye?".

"No yet Hugo, I've to go down to the Polis station at 7pm when Detective Moriarty starts his shift and get it back then".

"Ah, I see. So what kinda things were they asking you then in the interviews Simon?".

"Just about her family history and stuff in case something leaped out at them as to why somebody would've wanted to kill her".

"Like what bud?".

"Well I know her Mum got sexually assaulted by her Dad's best friend one night. They borrowed £5000 off of him once and when they went to his house about a year later to pay him back, her Mum went to bed early after a few drinks. Her Dad's best friend crept into bed with her and wanted his £5000 back in other ways. Her Mum only ever told Marie about that, who obviously told me, so it could possibly be him out for revenge".

"She also has an alcoholic Aunty who beat up her Gran once, about three months before her Gran died. The poor old Woman who was 80 odd woke up from an unconscious state with her own daughter on top of her in a drunken rage. Again, Marie knew about that too as her Gran had confided in her before she died. It could possibly be her Aunt that killed Marie in another drunken rage".

"Wow, fucked up family mate. You'll be glad you're out of that now?".

"Och there's plenty more than that and I'll save them for a rainy day. All they do is keep secrets from each other. The Polis are truly at a blank at the minute. The best man has been checked out too but he's just a fantasist loser. They've found some interesting stuff on him though during their enquiries and he'll be getting a chap at his door very soon about other stuff".

"Right mate, you've gave me the confidence to get back amongst the ladies again. I'm going to get down to Rose the hairdresser and get her to give me a shave, a haircut and wan of they man pampers yous all keep going on about these days and see if I can get myself a woman again. Safe trip home pal".

"Cheers Hugo!! Tell the lovely Rose I was asking after her and I'm sorry I couldn't get in for one of her special pampers".

"Will do pal!!"

Hugo heads out of Healy's with a spring in his step and off to Rose's to get pampered. Simon heads back over to the bar to speak to his Mum. The visitors from Gibraltar arrive tomorrow and it's Marie's funeral. Another busy day for the town coming up.

CHAPTER EIGHT

SOMETHING DOESN'T SIT RIGHT WITH ME

"Has anybody heard from Mel since she's been away" asks Babs.

"No, not a peep" says Clare.

"You'd think she'd update her Social Media and that if she was away backpacking eh?" says Lisa.

"Aye, all very odd that she's basically just disappeared off the face of the planet" said Kirsty.

"Mibee that's what she wanted, just to get away from everything and doesn't want to be bothered" said Jan.

"Aye true, it's just awfy weird that she just left like that though without saying goodbye to anybody" says Debbie.

"Ye never know what's going through folks heeds lassies" says Terry.

"Something just doesn't sit right with me" said Donna.

"Where's Bonnie the day Terry?" shouts Jan.

"It's Marie's funeral remember, she was her only pal really so felt that she had to go".

"Och shite aye" says Jan.

Terry's phone goes off.

"Hello!!"

"Oh Hello Russell!!"

"Oh that's grand, so they should be here by 12?"

"Great, I'll see you then".

"Right lassies that was Russell from Phoenix Taxi's. Our new arrivals from Gibraltar will be here for 12pm. Yous can all have an early lunch at 11.30am so I can show our new visitors round an empty factory first and then I'll bring them to Healy's".

"Woop Woop!!" shouts Kirsty.

11.35 and the lassies walk into Healy's and Bonnie is sitting in the corner with a few folk dressed in black and Jan motions her over to the snug.

"How'd it go hen?" says Jan.

"Och there wasn't a massive turn out for the poor lassie. She was kinda like the plague round here after what she did but it was a nice service for her".

"Och that's lovely darling" says Babs.

"How come yous are in so early anyway?" says Bonnie.

"We've got those guys coming over from Gibraltar today for the big visit. They should be here any minute" says Lisa.

"Oh shit aye, I forgot about that" says Bonnie.

"I'm riding the fit wan" shouts Jan.

Teresa comes from out of the back office and walks into the snug.

"Ladies, I want to have my Hen Night out soon because I'm getting bigger by the minute here. I don't want to travel too far in case something happens with the baby. What about Largs or something girls?".

"Largs?" says Clare.

"Yes Clare, Largs. I think that would be an excellent wee night away for us all ladies".

"It's a pity the Metro still isn't open eh Donna?" says Kirsty.

"Oh aye Teresa, we'd have hud you on those one pound shots for sure!!" says Donna.

"Well girls, there'll be no drinking for me with the way I am. I'll leave everything else up to yous".

Teresa heads back to the office.

Donna heads to the bar for the drinks.

"Tina can we all have our usual in the snug please and did Simon get away ok?" says Donna.

"Yes he did doll and of course hen I'll bring them over".

"You coming to Largs for Teresa's hen do Tina?" says Donna.

"Fucking Largs says Donald?".

Only Donald and his brother are at the bar for their usual lunch time pints.

"Fucks it to do with you Donald?" says Tina.

Donald just puts his heed doon whilst his brother is stood behind him growling at Tina.

"Don't you fucking growl at me ya wee tit or I'll come oor that bar and fling you aboot like an empty trackie son" says Tina to his serious looking brother.

"Sorry about them Tina" says Donna.

"Och don't apologise for them hen, it was fuck all to do with them. Of course I'll be there, I'll speak to JJ when yous have the dates and I'll take it off. I'm sure Sandra or JJ won't mind covering me here".

"Sorted" says Donna.

The pub starts to fill up with the regulars so JJ gives Tina a wee hand behind the bar. John, Colin and Tony are in along with Donald and his brother. Marie's family are in for her wake too so the pub is quite busy. Alberto has made a nice spread for the wake so they're all tucking into that.

This guy walks into the pub who nobody recognises so everybody turns round.

"Pint of your finest lager please Tina hen!!" says the handsome chap.

"Hugo? Is that you son?" says Tina.

"It sure fucking is hen!!".

"Wit the fucks happened to you man?" says Colin.

"I had a pep talk fae Simon yesterday and decided to give myself a shake folks. I went down to the lovely Rose's for one of they man pamper things. She shaved me, gave me this cracking new hair do and then a lovely Indian Head Massage as well. It was the fucking tits man and here I am. The new and improved Hugo!".

"Go and get me some eh they sausage rolls fae that buffet Donna" says Jan.

"Away tae fuck you ya brass neck" says Donna.

The doors of the pub swing open and in walks Terry with two tanned Gentlemen. She walks straight over to the snug to introduce them to all the Factory Girls.

Hugo's ears prick up and he watches on with interest as he takes a sip of his first beer in 20 odd years.

"Ladies, this is Alan Hartley and Jonny Olivera-Kenyon Jnr.

Hugo spits the sip of his pint out.

"Something wrong wi that pint Hugo"? says Tina.

"Naw Tina, naw".

CHAPTER NINE

I CANNY FUCKING BELIEVE IT MAN

Hugo takes another couple of sips of his pint and walks outside and takes his mobile phone out. He scrolls down to B and looks for Bruno and presses dial.

After a couple of rings Bruno picks up the phone.

"Hola".

"Bruno is that you man, it's Hugo!!".

"Huuuuuuuuuuuuugo!! I'm on way up to Malaga Airport to collect Simon, is everything ok Amigo?".

"No not really mate. What was the name of that Bank Manager in Gibraltar we kidnapped for the bank job pal?".

"I'm driving man, let me just pull in to this Service Station and I'll Google it amigo, I can't remember".

"This boy is his fucking double Bruno and I'm sure he has the same name".

"Ermmmm, it was Jonny Olivera-Kenyon according to Google, Hugo" says Bruno.

"I canny fucking believe it man!!".

"What's the matter Hugo?".

"His son, his fucking son is here in my home town and he's literally about 50ft away from me through a wall Bruno".

"Remain calm Hugo, he'll know about what happened to his Dad obviously but he never had any kids then so the boy wasn't even born. We done extensive research on him and he was a single man back then. He has no clue about you or shouldn't do anyway".

"As soon as I saw the wee cunt his face rang a bell. You're right Bruno mate, I just still always look over my shoulder when I leave the house, I'm still paranoid pal that's all. You better go and collect Simon, Amigo. Get him to text me when yous get back to La Linea pal".

"I will do Hugo, great to hear from you my Amigo".

The phone goes dead and Hugo walks back into the pub.

"Are you alright Hugo?" says Tina.

"Aye hen, I was just making sure the driver was going up to the airport for your Simon".

"You look like you've seen a ghost son".

"Aye, mibee I have Tina. Mibee I have".

"So lassies, now all the introductions are out the way, if yous would like to head back over to the Factory and crack on with the order, I'll get the gentlemen a wee drink to get them settled and then I'll bring them over" said Terry.

Terry walks over to the bar with the two visitors.

"This is my son and my soon to be daughter in law's bar gents, so whatever you'd like to drink is on the house.

"I'll just have a half lager" said Alan.

"I'll have a nice Scottish Whisky on the rocks please" says Jonny Jnr.

Tina pours the drinks and Hugo canny take his eyes off Jonny Jnr.

"A Whisky son? Does your Maw and Da know yer oot this late wee man?" said Tony.

Jonny Jnr looks at Terry.

"Can you translate what he just said please?".

"Just ignore him Jonny Jnr".

"Oh ok" he says whilst tentatively sniggering.

An old fat grey guy dressed in a black suit, white shirt and black tie on walks over to bar to order some drinks. It's the recently departed Marie's Dad. JJ knows that Tina's son was married to his daughter so heads over to serve him to save the awkwardness.

"What can I get you Sir?" says JJ.

"Eh just the same again for my table please JJ".

"No bother, by the way, I'm sorry to hear about Marie, she came in here quite a bit recently".

"Och thanks JJ son. It's still a bit of a shock to the system but we'll get there".

"She was a fucking cow!!" shouts Tony.

All hell breaks loose at the bar. Colin and John grab Tony, the old man is restrained by Hugo. Marie's family look over and a tall specky boy walks over trying to get involved too. Turns out he's Marie's brother. Donald and his brother grab him.

This isn't what Terry wanted on her visitors first day in the town and they both look quite shaken up by it all. JJ puts Tony out the bar and tells him he's barred. Colin and John escort him away. Hugo, Donald and his brother escort the other two back to their family at the other side of the bar.

Alberto comes out of the kitchen with a rolling pin in his hand asking if they need any assistance.

Teresa comes out of the back office and goes straight behind the bar to confront JJ.

"What in God's name has just happened JJ, I heard an almighty argument there from inside the office".

"Och drunk Tony said something to Marie's Dad at the bar and it all kicked off. The lads at the bar sorted it darling. Go back to the office baby, it's done".

"I just knew something was going to get said in here today JJ" says Tina. "I thought somebody was going to say something to me about my Simon but it had to be Tony. Canny hold his ain pish when he's had a drink".

"Don't worry about it Tina, it's done now and he's barred. I'll let Sandra know as well".

Terry and her two visitor's from Gibraltar finish off their drinks and head over to the Factory. The funeral crowd have ate most of the buffet and decide to move on to another bar in case there's another scene. The mad lunch time rush settles and JJ leaves Tina at the Bar with just Hugo left.

"Christ that was some start to yer shift there Tina" says Hugo.

"Aye, I knew something would happen or get said".

Just at that, Hugo's phone goes off. It's a Text.

"Hugo, it's Simon. That's me arrived back in the Costa Del Sol and currently in Bruno's Ferrari heading back to La Linea. If you see my Maw can you let her know I've arrived safely mate? Have a good one pal!!" Si x

"Tina that was your Simon. That's him arrived back safely".

"Oh good, he did the right thing getting away from here".

CHAPTER TEN

ANOTHER BODY

Terry gets back to the Factory with Alan and Jonny and starts to give them the guided tour. They're very impressed with the cleanliness of the place and how hard the lassies are working to get their order out. Terry takes them up to her office where you can look down to the shop floor from her huge window.

"They all seem to be having a good time down there", says Alan.

"Yes, they all get on very well Alan. They work hard and play hard. I don't stop them having a laugh, I used to be down there and a happy work place is what you want".

"Are we ok to have a look around the rest of the factory now Terry?" says the young Jonny Jnr.

"Yes of course, let's go!".

She takes them down to the shop floor and shows them the girls working on the order. She takes them past the toilets to head outside.

"There's an awful smell coming from the Ladies toilets there Terry" says Jonny Jnr.

"Yes, we have a man in now fixing them as the girls had been complaining about a smell recently, that's why that sign is up on the door".

Terry takes them outside to the stunning grounds and car park. Sirens can be heard in the distance. They're getting closer and closer. Two Police cars screetch into the car park and come to a halt. Detective Moriarty and his partner get out of one vehicle and two burly Men get out the other.

"Terry!"

"Yes Detective Moriarty".

"Can I talk to you in private please?"

"Of course you can, what's the matter?"

"The plumber who's been working in your Ladies toilet traced the bad smell that's been filtering through into the Ladies toilets. He went down to the old abandoned store room in the basement and it's not good news I'm afraid".

"Why, why, what's happened?" screams Terry.

"He's found a female body in there".

"No, it can't be".

"I'm afraid so, grab the girls and lock the Factory up until we investigate further Terry".

Terry rushes inside and quickly explains to the Girls what's happened and rushes them over to Healy's. The Police tape off the area surrounding the old abandoned store room and start their investigation.

Meanwhile, back at Healy's in the snug.

"What the actual fuck man?" says Jan.

"I know" says Lisa.

"Has anybody seen Bonnie? She was with the funeral entourage. Somebody call her!" says Babs.

" Babs, it canny be Bonnie, that smell has been coming out of there a few weeks now" says Debbie.

"I'll call her anyway" says Terry.

"Wit the fuck has happened to this toon man?" says Donna.

"It's definitely getting worse" says Kirsty.

"Wit aboot Mel?" says Clare.

"Do you know what Clare, that's not a bad call that" says Jan.

News of the body starts to filter around the town, and the hub of the town "Healy's" soon starts to fill up. Within a couple of hours, all the regulars are in.

"BeJesus JJ, it's absolutely terrible news this isn't it? I think we should seriously tink about heading back to Ireland. Dis is no place to bringing up our new babby for sure".

"Teresa, there hasn't been a murder here for 25 years and now there's been two in the past few weeks. Let the Police do their job, they'll catch whoever's responsible for this".

Sandra comes in to start her shift and Tina decides to stay on and help her as the pub is mobbed. The National press are in town as well again and this wee toon is gripped by murder fever.

Detective Moriarty and his colleague enter the pub and head to the Bar.

"Is JJ and Teresa in Sandra?".

"Aye Detective, they're through the back".

They start to walk through to the back office and the pub falls silent as everybody watches them go through.

There's a knock at JJ & Teresa's office door.

"Come in!" shouts Teresa.

"Ah Detective's, what can we do for you this evening" asks JJ.

"We know the identity of the body that's been discovered today over at the Factory. It's Mel and she's been murdered the exact same way as Marie was. Two stab wounds to the neck and a slashed throat".

"Oh my God!" screams Teresa.

"Yes, I'm afraid so" says Detective Moriarty. "We're about to release a statement to the Press and it looks like we a Serial Killer loose in the town".

The Detective's leave the bar to the waiting Press and camera's everywhere. They walk towards the already set up microphones whilst everybody in the pub watches the Press Conference on the TV from inside the pub. Detective Moriarty walks towards the microphones.

"Ladies and Gentlemen, I can confirm that we have found a female body in the abandoned store-room in the Textile's Factory. We can also confirm that the lady was Melanie Jones who used to work in the bar behind me. Her family have been informed".

"I'd don't want to raise fear and alarm at this stage but more vigilance. The way in which this lady has met her grizzly end has the same hallmarks of the woman who washed up on our shores a week ago. It looks like we have a Serial Killer in amongst us Ladies and Gentlemen".

"The last thing I want to say is that both deaths have resulted in two puncture wounds to the neck and a slashed throat. If this method refreshes anyones mind or you have any information that may help us with this case then please call me direct on 01294 461055. Thank you".

Back in Healy's.

"Wit the actual Fuck man!!" says Hugo. "This is fucking unreal man".

"Aye terrible. I liked Mel in here and couldn't believe it when she just left like that, now this explains everything" says Colin.

"But didn't she leave a letter?" says John.

Donna is stood beside John and hears this.

"That's it John!!" says Donna.

"What?"

"The Letter!!" says Donna.

Donna rushes through to the back office and bangs on JJ's office door.

"Donna, what can I do for you?" says JJ.

"The letter, the letter!!" she screams. "Do you still have the letter that Mel left for yous when she was supposed to go away?".

"We do Donna, it'll be in her file in the filing cabinet there" says Teresa.

"Ok, don't touch it whatever you do, and phone Detective Moriarty. It's not from Mel, it's from her killer".

"Eh?" says JJ.

"Well she never ever left the Toon. Whoever has killed her has tried to cover his or her tracks by sending yous a letter. Phone him now, it's from the killer I'm telling you".

"Teresa gets on the phone right away to Detective Moriarty".

The Police come round and take Mel's full file away for analysis and to study the letter. Has Donna's quick thinking brought about the demise of this small towns Serial Killer?

CHAPTER ELEVEN

A WEEKEND OF FEAR

It's been a pretty mental week again in the Toon and with Mel's murder now alongside Marie's, the town is on edge. JJ calls a staff meeting with Teresa, Tina and Sandra. Saturday is always the busiest day and JJ doesn't expect anything different today.

"Ladies, before the pub opens today I wanted to have a quick chat about recent events. Obviously Mel is very close to the punters hearts, let's just carry on as normal in here this weekend and try to make it a safe and enjoyable environment for our locals".

"JJ, everybody is shiteing it" says Sandra.

"I know Sandra, don't worry, I've spoken to Russell and you'll get staff taxi's to and from work now until this killer is caught. I'll look after yous in here so don't worry about a thing pal".

"It's all pretty surreal" says Tina. I've been in this Toon 60 years now and never seen anything like this. I hope the dirty bastard gets caught soon".

"Ladies just be vigilant is all I'm saying. If the killer drinks in here then listen to conversations. See if he or she slips up in any way. Yous can be the eyes and ears for the Police in here. Any little information whatsoever might nail this person".

"JJ's right Ladies, loose lips sink ships and all that and you know what the punters are like sometimes after a few" says Teresa.

The ladies leave the office and start to open the pub up. Everybody will be on edge and it's down to them to keep the punters in good spirits.

Terry is the first to walk in with her two visitors and takes them straight into the snug.

"Guys, I hope the past few days haven't put you off us completing your order for yous?".

"No not all. We're very impressed with your community spirit here and your Factory Girls" says Alan.

"It's not your fault that the killer dropped the body there Terry. He or she just might have previous knowledge of the building that's all. My Dad was a Bank Manager and his bank got robbed 20 odd years ago in Gibraltar and it was an inside job. It's usually people that you know" says Jonny.

"Do you know what Jonny? That's a good point that lad" says Alan.

"Well yes you might have a point there son. The thing is, it's only been women that've worked there over the years" says Terry.

"Has it always been a Textiles Factory Terry?" asks Jonny.

"Nooooooooooooo" says Terry.

"It actually used to originally be a Slaughterhouse for pigs owned by a certain Mr Longshanks before but it got shut down for lots of Health and Safety breaches.

Most of our male punters in here worked there back in the day".

"Ah, I see" says Alan.

The pub starts to fill up with all the boys who are all talking about the Football coupons and the Horse Racing bets they've put on. Colin and John have got their usual accumulator on.

"Right Colin, wit three teams did you pick again?" says John.

"Sellik, Killie and Cowdenbeath" says Colin.

"Fucking Cowdenbeath ya bampot?" says John.

"Aye fucking Cowdenbeath, who's your three then?" says Colin.

"Partick Thistle, Ayr United and Dumbarton" says John.

"Ayr yefucking Nited? Efter the fucking last time ya dick?" says Colin.

There's two notable absentees from the male contingency at the bar today. The barred Tony and Donald's brother Pedro. Tina digs a wee bit more.

"Where's Pedro the day Donald?" says Tina.

"Och he's no coming oot this weekend, says he's skint. I said I'd take him oot but he said no".

"Well he was an arsehole to me the other day in here growling away at me. If he starts any of his shite, he'll be like Tony and put oot that door for good".

"I'll let him know Tina".

"Right boys, we'd better get out of "Sadie's Snug" cause the Factory Girls will be in soon and this is where they all sit. It's the closest bit to the dancefloor. Oh and Jan will eat yous both for breakfast so come on over to the bar and I'll introduce to the boys".

"Did you say Jan? Who's Jan? says Jonny.

"Oh you'll find out soon enough son haha" says Terry.

They head over to the bar.

"Gents, this is Alan and this is Jonny. They're visitors from Gibraltar so please be nice to them and make them feel welcome. This is Hugo, Colin, John and over there is Donald".

"Pleased to meet yous" is the cry from everyone.

"So guys, Terry was telling me that the Textiles Factory used to be a Slaughterhouse for pigs" says Alan.

"That's right, Donald over there, and me worked in the Packing Hall. Colin worked in the Washing Room that hosed the pigs down after slaughter. Hugo here never worked there and the other two that are normally here, Tony and Pedro, worked there too" says John.

"Oh how come you never worked there then Hugo" asks Jonny.

"Why don't you mind yer ain fucking business son".

Young Jonny puts his head down in submission.

"Och Hugo has always been a Professional Gambler son. He doesn't mean anything by it" said Colin.

The doors swing open and in walk the Factory Girls. Everybody barring Clare who's away playing Fitba as usual. She'll join up the lassies tonight.

"Right Donna, it's your round" shouts Kirsty.

"I'll give you a haun carrying them over" says Jan.

"Donna, Jan". "How's it gaun?".

"Aye no bad Hugo".

"Wit were ye coming oot of JJ's office last night with the Polis fir Donna?" asks Hugo.

"The boys were talking about Mel and the letter she sent the Pub saying that she'd gone backpacking when obviously she never left the Toon. It just clicked with me that it must've been the killer that sent it so I put two and two together and got Teresa to contact the Police".

"Did JJ & Teresa still have the letter?" asks Hugo.

"Aye, it was in her file in the filing cabinet" said Donna.

"Good work Chief Inspector Taggart!!" chuckles Hugo.

"You back on the booze again Hugo? Oh and by the way, I like the new hair-do and clean shaven face these days" said Jan.

"Indeed I am back on the booze Jan and thank you".

"Where did this change all come from then?"

"Och it was when Simon was oor, he said for me not to dwell on stuff and start living my life again so I've taken his advice. Fuck it. Ching Ching ladies".

The boys are watching the Fitba and the Horse Racing and the lassies are in the snug drinking shots and having a laugh. Auld Jimmy that runs the Disco and the Karaoke equipment starts loading all of equipment into the pub. All talk of a Serial Killer being let loose on the town has been forgotten.

For now.

CHAPTER TWELVE

ON YERSEL HUGO

The Party in Healy's is in full swing, the Karaoke is blasting out and even a few News Reporters who are staying in the local B&B's are in to join in with the craic.

Babs is up with Lisa singing a duet to "Dirty Old Town" which is probably convenient at the minute with all that's going on. Clare has joined the rest of the girls but got a sore one at the Fitba so there'll be no dancing for her later.

At the bar, Colin & John are happy because their coupon came in, even with Cowdenbeath and Ayr on it. Donald is sat at one end of the bar with Jonny Jnr and Hugo is chatting away to auld Alan from Gibraltar.

Teresa has joined Terry and the rest of the lassies in the snug but with only one month to go until she gets married to JJ and two months to go until she gives birth, there's no way she'll touch a drop.

"Have ye's sorted Largs out yet girls" says Teresa.

"Yes we have Teresa, we're going next Friday night" says Terry.

"Ah bless ya's girls" says Teresa.

"There's eleven of us going up in the minibus Teresa, the seven girls on the day shift at the Factory, me, Terry, yourself and Tina from behind the bar and the B&B is already booked" says Bonnie.

"Ah brilliant, it'll be great craic sure" says Teresa.

The bar door opens and in walks Pedro with somebody that everyone didn't think they'd ever see in Healy's. Longshanks!! They make their way over to Donald and Jonny Jnr and go to order some drinks.

"Evening Tina" says Longshanks.

"Erm evening Mr Longshanks, what can I get yous?".

Longshanks owns a lot of businesses in the town and isn't well liked. Tina was his PA in the Slaughterhouse that he owned years ago and she still calls him Mr Longshanks.

"I'll have three pints of lager please and a whisky is it, for the young man as well, that's stood beside Donald".

He pulls out a crisp £50 note and puts it on the bar.

"Just keep the change there Tina".

"He's a smug bastard that cunt" says Colin.

"I keep hearing yous say the word Cunt quite a lot in here Hugo. What does it mean?" says Alan.

"Well it means a lot of things Alan my friend. It's a term of endearment here in Scotland, but down the road in England it's very offensive. I'll give you some examples".

"Here's a Scottish Guide to the Word Cunt".

Good Cunt = Nice Person

Daft Cunt = Silly Person

Thick Cunt = Stupid Person

Bunch of Cunts = Tories

That Cunt = Him/Her

Total Cunt = Tommy Robinson

Kick his Cunt in = Fight That Man

And Finally

Ooo Ya Cunt = That's sore

"I think that covers it Alan, yer sorted now pal" says Hugo.

"Cheers Hugo, you're a good Cunt you haha".

Longshanks gives Donald & Pedro their Pints and young Jonny Jnr his Whisky.

"I thought you weren't coming out this weekend? says Donald.

"Aye well I wiznae but when yer auld boss phone's ye, ye canny say naw cun ye?".

"Well I'm yer brother ya prick and ye said naw to me".

"Good evening young man, I haven't seen you around here before". "What's your name"? says Longshanks.

"Ermmmm Jonny Olivera-Kenyon Jnr Sir".

"That's not a name from around these parts young man".

"Yes, myself and my friend over there talking to Hugo, are guests of Terry at the Textiles Factory. We placed a big order with them and wanted to see it with our own eyes getting produced".

"Ah I see, myself and Terry go way back. It's a shame what happened there finding that body eh?".

"Yes, indeed it was".

"Wits that prick Longshanks dain in here Terry?" says Jan.

"Och he's free to drink in here if he pleases. He never got his wish to get his hands on the Factory or the Bar and nor will he ever. Leave him be" said Terry.

After a couple of more hours the party is in full swing. Everybody is up on the dancefloor barring Longshanks, Donald & Pedro from the boys side and Teresa is keeping Clare company who's got her ankle in a bucket of ice.

The slow songs are starting to come on now and Hugo is up there slow dancing with Jan absolutely steaming oot his nut.

"Oan yersell Hugo!!" shouts Colin.

CHAPTER THIRTEEN

A VITAL LEAD IN THE CASE

"Cup a tea Hugo?" says Jan.

"Wit the Fuck man?" says Hugo.

"Ye wurnae saying that at five o'clock this morning" says Jan.

"Aww fur fuck sake man. Wit fucking happened here?".

"Wit didnae happen mare like? Ye took twenty years of frustrations oot on me last night big boy. Ye were like a Bull in a China shop".

"Oafft fur fuck sake Jan!!".

Jan flicks the telly on and the Scottish News is about to come on.

"Thanks to Judith Ralston for the Weather and now over to Jackie Bird for the National News".

"There's been a major breakthrough in the Serial Killer case down in Ayrshire, where two women were found dead with the same injuries, let's cross over now to our Kilmarnock studio, where Detective Moriarty is live".

"Detective, what more can you tell us?".

"Well Jackie, we came across a letter that the killer sent trying to cover his or her tracks and from that letter we've came across some vital clues. First of all the killer has the spelling of a seven year old, we also got finger prints and the killer's DNA. We've also managed to obtain through said DNA that the person is indeed a man that we're looking for".

"Wow that's a major breakthrough for yourself and your team".

"It is indeed Jackie, we just want to let the killer know that the net is closing in on you now and we will catch you".

"Och that's fucking excellent news Jan eh".

"It is that, I hope they catch the bastard soon. Any idea who it could be Hugo?".

"Honestly pal, I've got no clue, I'm baffled".

"Aye me too Hugo, me too".

Kirsty heads up to Sammy's Store and to cash in her voucher that she won on the Radio.

"Morning Sammy".

"Ah morning Kirsty" says Sammy.

"Can I just get hunners of chocolate and biscuits with this voucher please Sammy and I'll take it into work for the lassies".

"Aye nae bother Kirsty. Fill yer boots pal".

Pedro walks in and whilst Kirsty is at the Paper stand he grabs a copy of every single newspaper.

"Fuck me Pedro, wan paper no enough for you?" says Kirsty.

"Och I like to read them and do the crosswords in them".

"Oh ok Pedro".

Debbie walks in to Sammy's.

"Morning Sammy, Pedro and oh hiya Kirsty".

"Hiya pal" says Kirsty.

"I'm jist in for the papers Kirsty".

"That's if there's any left. That Pedro just bought one of every single one the mad eejit".

JJ and Teresa are lying in bed having a well earned long lie on a Sunday morning.

"Are you looking forward to your Hen Night in Largs on Friday my Princess?"

"I am indeed JJ. How come you're not having a Stag do?"

"Och when I asked Hugo to be my best man, I told him I didn't want one because he wasn't drinking at the time. It wouldn't have been the same".

"Ah that's fair enough sure, I'm sure he'd be up for one now haha".

"Yeah true but I'll still give it a miss I think. Are you looking forward to all the Irish clan coming over for the wedding?"

"Of course I am JJ, it'll be great craic sure".

"Aye I know, I just canny wait to see them all".

Babs, Lisa, and Donna arranged to pop round to Clare's last night to make sure she was alright this morning after her swollen ankle yesterday.

"Och thanks for coming round lassies but I'm fine. I get wan of these every weekend" says Clare.

"Are ye sure yer ok darling" says Babs.

"Honestly Babs, I'm hunky dory, I'll be round Healy's later".

"I was jist about to ask you that there" says Lisa.

"Did yous see the news this morning lassies?" says Donna.

"Aye" says Clare. "Good on you for that quick spot with the letter thing Donna". "That could be the actual thing that catches him".

"Oh I hope so lassies. We need to keep going about in groups to give the bastard no chance of getting one of us".

"Aye" says Lisa.

Alan and Jonny Jnr are sat at the B&B breakfast table and contemplating what to do with their day today.

"I can't remember getting home last night Jonny, can you?" says Alan.

"Yes, the three of us came back in a Taxi driven by a lovely guy named Russell" says Jonny.

"The three of us"? says Alan.

"Yes, I brought a lovely girl back last night. Bonnie I think she said her name was".

"Ah, good on you my boy. Where is she now Jonny?"

"Oh, she um did what she had to do and left".

"What do you want to do today Jonny?"

"Well Bonnie said something about a "Sunday Sesh" in Healy's today. I'm not quite sure what that is but I'm up for it anyway".

"Ah you're young lad. You go and enjoy yourself, I think I'll go a nice walk along that shore front".

It looks like everybody is geared up for a good old Sunday session in Healy's except old Alan. He has other plans. After his breakfast he gets changed and sets off for a nice long walk along the shore front.

He gets about a mile into his walk and there's absolutely nobody about. He stops by a group of builder's on the shore front who are working on a new building.

"Hiya lads, this building looks impressive, what's this going to be then?"

"Oh it's going to be a Spanish style Bar/Cafe we've been told. All very posh inside with a roof terrace looking over the Sea" says one of the builders.

"Very nice boys, very nice. Have a great day chaps!"

Old Alan continues on with his walk, taking in the beautiful of the Isle of Arran and Ailsa Craig.

He's walking along the beach when he sees a figure in the distance. It looks like a young woman sleeping. As he gets closer he goes up to her to waken her up. She's not sleeping, she's dead!!

CHAPTER FOURTEEN

WE'RE MOVING TO IRELAND

News filters round the town that another female body has been found dead. Old Alan is with the Police down at the Station just now giving his statement. Everybody else is in Healy's.

"What happened Jonny?" says Tina.

"I don't know, I was having breakfast with Alan and I told him I was coming here to meet all of you guys, he told me he was going for a walk. That's all I know".

"Right who's fucking missing?" says Jan.

The group have a scan round. The only people missing are Teresa, as JJ told her to go back to bed and take today off, Donald and Pedro who don't come in on a Sunday and Bonnie but she's never in until tea time as she always has a long lie on a Sunday.

"Right, looks like nobody we know is missing so it might be some poor bugger from the next town" says Clare.

"The news will be on in a minute so we should know more then" says Terry.

"What time did you say Bonnie normally comes in guys? I'm supposed to be meeting her here but she's not answering her phone" says Jonny.

"Och don't worry about Bonnie young man, she's a free spirit and sleeps most of a Sunday so she'll get here when she gets here" says Babs.

The National News comes on and everybody falls silent.

"Murder number three in Seaside Serial Killer Town!!"

"I'm Jackie Bird and here is your National News".

"Another woman has been found murdered this morning in the West Coast of Scotland". Let's cross over to our Kilmarnock studio where we're joined by Detective Moriarty once more".

"Detective, you told us the last time that the net was closing in on your Serial Killer but yet you find another body this morning".

"Jackie yes we did and it is. At the minute we don't know the identity of the young lady but she does bear the same injuries as the other two women who have been found in the town".

"The only thing I can tell the public right now is that she has long brown hair, approximately 25 and was wearing a purple dress with black boots on and if anybody is missing anyone with that description or seen anybody out with that on last night then please contact myself at the station".

"Bonnie!!" screams Jonny.

"Noooooooooooooooo!!" screams Terry.

JJ phones Detective Moriarty and confirms who the body is. The Detective comes to the Bar to clear young Jonny as his DNA would be on her body. He takes the young man down to the station anyway for a statement where he meets up with old Alan.

JJ takes his Mum to his house so she can sit with Teresa. She's too distraught to be on her own today. Teresa just can't believe the news she's just heard as she's woken up by them coming in.

"What? Really JJ?" she says. "Once this wedding and baby are done, we're moving to Ireland!!".

"What?" says Terry.

"Mum, she's just woken up and heavily pregnant, she doesn't know what she's saying right now".

"Oh I fecking do JJ!!".

"Did you just swear baby? Awwwwwww".

"Don't fecking Awwwwwww me".

Meanwhile back at Healy's Tina sees Hugo approaching the bar.

"Pint Hugo?"

"Aye a pint of fucking water Tina!"

"Ye no drinking the day son?"

"Drinking? It's the fucking devils juice a tell ye!"

"Get a drink doon ye Hugo ya fanny. What's the worst that can happen?" shouts Jan.

The last two murders made it on to Local and Scottish National News but now it's gone even bigger. Sky has it as their Breaking News item and everyone in the pub is glued to the screen.

"Good afternoon, this is Kay Burley with some Breaking News! There's been a third murder in the space of a few weeks in a once sleepy village on the West Coast of Scotland. There's talk of a Serial Killer on the loose. Let's cross over live to our new Crime Correspondent, Niall Paterson. Niall, what can you tell us?".

"Well Kay, I come from a village about 20 miles South of here and we've never heard the like of this ever round these parts. I'm joined by local Detective, Detective Moriarty. What can you tell us this afternoon Detective?".

"Well Niall, what I can tell you is that the victim was at a local Hotel with a friend and left that hotel around 4am to walk home on her own. The victim was pounced upon and received two puncture wounds to the neck and a slashed throat. Identical to the two other victims that we've had recently".

"What leads if any, do you have at the moment Detective?".

"All we know is that he's male, we have his finger prints and DNA and that he can't spell very well. We assume he's a local man as all of the victims knew each other. We will catch him soon but we ask that all the ladies in the area remain vigilant and don't walk about on your own until we catch him".

"Well Kay it's a frightening time here for the locals and the Police are doing everything in their power to catch this cold blooded Killer. It looks like with the evidence they have so far, his time might be running out. Back to the studio".

Meanwhile in Sadies Snug.

"This is getting madder by the minute man" says Lisa.

"It is darling but I'm sure the Police will catch him soon now" said Babs.

"I have an idea lassies" says Clare. "I can do a Hidden Team for my Fitba team. Get Tina to pass it round all the guys in the pub and maybe one of their finger prints matches the killer's.

"I like that, it's gotta be worth a shot lassies" says Debbie.

"Lets start collecting DNA as well lassies" says Kirsty. "I know it's bogging but try and get a hair off all the guys in here and we'll hand them over to the Police. Run your fingers through their hair when you're at the bar for drinks and stuff".

"Well I've got plenty of Hugo's fae last night lassies. Some of them are still stuck in my teeth haha".

"Jaaaaaaaaaaan" shouts Donna.

"Lassies, I think we can crack this case ourselves. Let's do it for our fellow sisters that've departed us. Especially oor Bonnie. I'll speak to Tina about that old Slaughterhouse as she was Longshank's PA back then I'm sure. It didn't get shut down for nothing. I bet that place hides a lot of secrets!!"

The Factory Girls are buzzing now and have the bit between their teeth. They think they have a great chance of cracking this case themselves. There's seven of them on it and with Hugo ruled out straight away with his history, the lassies get to work. They know the Police will have all of his fingerprints and DNA and there's no way Jan let him out of her sight all last night. This is a game changer. Can the lassies come up Trumps?

CHAPTER FIFTEEN

TERESA'S HEN DO

Thankfully the town has been quiet all week and the Serial Killer has been laying low. The lassies have spent the week collecting hair samples from local guys and the Hidden Team in the pub is nearly full. All the lassies are round at Rose the Hairdresser's getting their hair done and pampered for Teresa's Hen do tonight in Largs.

All the girls arrive at Rose's except Donna, Kirsty & Tina. They'll get done last. Donna & Kirsty are away round to Tina's to chat about the old Slaughterhouse to see if they can come up with any clues.

"Morning Donna. Morning Kirsty".

"Morning Tina" says both the lassies.

"Come in girls, come in" says Tina.

They walk into Tina's kitchen and there's two big boxes with dusty files inside.

"Wit are they Tina?" asks Kirsty.

"I kept the final year's files from the old Slaughterhouse and the reports from the Inspectors to see if it was of any use to yous. What is it you need them for anyway?".

"Ermm my boy is doing a project on it at the school Tina, so we're just trying to get as much information as possible about the place if that's ok?".

"Aye that's fine, take them away lassies, I don't know why I kept them all this time anyway".

"That's excellent Tina cheers" said Kirsty.

The lassies spend another hour at Tina's having a blether but they need to get to Rose's where all the rest of the lassies are waiting for them.

Rose is a lovely woman. She's been the resident Hairdresser in the toon for years. Always glam and happy and smiley. She's in her 50's but you could never tell. A blonde bombshell like Marilyn Monroe.

"Hiya lassies" says Rose. "Right let me get you all a cuppa first. I've drafted in the two Margaret's today as my little helpers and they'll start washing all your hair. So wits been happening then girls and where are yous off to tonight then?".

"It's me Hen do tonight Rose in Largs. There was supposed to be eleven of us going but with what happened to Bonnie, there's ten now".

"Why don't you come Rose? The room is booked anyway" says Terry.

"Och you wouldn't want me there lassies".

"Aye we would" says Babs.

"Och I'll let yous know later on, is that alright?"

"Of course" says Teresa.

Rose passes out all the cuppas to the girls and makes a start on all of their hair.

"So lassies, do yous all like my hair? I was growing it for Simon. I was hoping he wouldn't go back to Spain and just stay here with me but no joy. I live in hope though".

"It's lovely Rose, all long and curly" says Jan.

"It's a wee shame what happened to Bonnie eh?" says Rose.

"Aye it is that Rose" says Lisa. "She was a lovely lassie, a free spirit and then that bastard did that to her".

"Have you been busy this morning Rose"? asks Clare.

"I've only had that Donald's brother Pedro in this morning. He comes in every Friday morning so he does. He gies me the dry boak. Doesn't leave me alone. Gads. Oh that reminds me Margaret, can you sweep up his hair over by that chair please pal?".

"Oh I'll help you Margaret" says Jan.

Jan senses an opportunity here. Out of all the guys they know, it's just Pedro and Tony who's hair they don't have. Margaret sweeps up the hair and Jan gets down on her knees with the wee shovel. Once Margaret sweeps onto the shovel, Jan quickly graps a chunk of hair and wraps it in a wee bit of paper towel. Job done.

"Where's Donna, Kirsty & Tina?" says Rose.

"Oh they two are round at Tina's for a wee cuppa and a blether. They're going to pop round later so you're not too overcrowded in here" says Clare.

Rose finishes all the ladies off and decides to go to Largs with them all. They decide to meet up in Healy's for a drink before heading to Largs. Russell has put on a minibus for them for free to take them to Largs and bring them back tomorrow for the safety of the local women.

Russell walks into the pub to talk to Terry.

"Ok Terry, I've got eleven going and sixteen coming back tomorrow is that right?"

"Keep your voice down Russell, Teresa doesn't know about the five coming back with us".

"Ah right, sorry Terry".

The lassies finish their drinks in Healy's and pile on the bus and head up the coast to Largs. Russell drops them off at the famous Nardini's Ice Cream shop where you get the boat to Millport. They blindfold Teresa and lead her off the bus carefully. Terry has a big surprise for her.

"Careful ladies, careful" says Terry. Ok Teresa, you can take your blindfold off now.

"OH MY GOD!!!" screams Teresa. Mum, Bernadette, Frances, Margaret & Karen!! How? When?"

"Did you not think we'd make your Hen do now darling" says Teresa's Mum Mairead.

"Well I didn't, no".

"We wouldn't miss it for the World darling. All the men back home send their love and they said they'll see you next month at the wedding. Wow look at bump too".

"Yes, huge now Mum. Och it's so grand to see you all".

Teresa introduces everybody to each other. Terry & Mairead catch up too. All the ladies are in great spirits and they take Largs by storm. The Factory Girls have most of their evidence now as well and they're looking to hand it in to Detective Moriarty next week.

CHAPTER SIXTEEN

GOTCHA

The sixteen ladies filter off Russell's minibus. Only old Bernadette and Teresa were the ones who weren't drinking. The rest are in pretty bad shape and head into Healy's for a curer. Well, except Donna & Kirsty. They have other things on their mind. The two of them head round to Donna's to start going through the files from the Old Slaughterhouse.

"Right Kirsty, let's get through these pal. Never mind the actual Slaughterhouse files. Let's concentrate on the Inspector's reports".

"Good idea Donna" says Kirsty.

The two of them get to work and it's not long before Kirsty finds something interesting in one of the reports. Kirsty reads it out to Donna.

"One of the employees, "Peter Black" is in charge of slaughtering the pigs in the Killing Hall. His assistant "Tony McLeod" is in charge of stunning them first with a scissor like piece of equipment with two tennis balls on the end. Tony would sweep the legs of the pig to get it on the floor and then clamp said instrument around the head of the pig until it was stunned".

"Tony would then attach the stunned pigs leg to an ankle bracelet and then said pig would be raised up off the ground and go along a mechanical line approx 5ft off the ground along to "Peter Black" who would slit the pig's throat until it bled out".

"Is Peter Black not that creepy Pedro in the pub, Donald's brother?" says Donna.

"Aye that's him Donna. It doesn't make him the killer but slitting throats was as easy as 1,2,3 to him. Let's read on".

Donna is reading the other reports from the Inspector's too.

"I think I've something here as well Kirsty".

"Oh, what what, tell me".

Donna starts to read it out.

"All of the Departments in the Slaughterhouse are required to do written reports at the end of their shifts for the numbers that have came through the establishment on any given day. Every Departments reports were fine except for the Killing Hall. "Peter Black" had to submit a report at the end of every shift and his spelling was like that of a seven year old. His boss, Mr Longshanks, said "that they were used to it and kinda understood what he meant". We've attached one of his reports".

"Oh oh, let's see if his handwriting ties up with the letter sent to the Pub" says Kirsty.

The girls read on and on. There's hundreds of reports from the Inspectors. The girls are horrified at what they're reading. No wonder the place got shut down. There wasn't much Health and Safety back in the 1980's but some of the stuff is just cruelty.

"Gotcha ya fucking bastard!" screams Donna.

"What what what?" shouts Kirsty.

"We've got him Kirsty, we've got him. Wait till ye hear this!!"

"Upon interviewing all of the employees individually, testimony from two brothers, "Colin McLeod" and "John McLeod" revealed that they weren't happy with one of their colleagues but were told just to "shut their mouths and get on with their jobs" as they were the youngest members of staff.

"They both stated that the talk of the Slaughterhouse was always the last pig that came through the pen on a Friday would get some special treatment as it was nearly the weekend. Everybody had to stop what they were doing and attend the Killing Hall. The poor last pig wouldn't get the normal stunned treatment from their big brother "Tony" but when it got to "Peter Black", the mood changed. Tony wasn't allowed to stun it, just hang it up".

"Peter always used to get a kick out of it. Even Mr Longshanks would stand and applaud and cheer him on. As before the poor pig got it's throat slashed, "Pedro" as the boys called him, would give the pig two puncture wounds. First in the neck, and then slash it's throat. It was his signature move and then we all had to clap and cheer. It was sick!!"

"The fucking bastard!!" screams Kirsty.

"Right Kirsty, it's nearly 9pm now, let's get all this evidence. His spelling mistakes, the Report, these interviews from Colin & John, the hair from the Salon and the Hidden Team from the Pub. I noticed he'd taken a Team so his fingerprints will be on that too".

"Let's nail this bastard now Donna. Straight to Detective Moriarty".

The ladies gather up all of their evidence and fire round to Healy's. Donna says to Kirsty to get all the Factory Girls into the Snug which she does.

"Right lassies, between us all, I think we've cracked this Serial Killer case. Jan, have you still got that hair from hairdresser's yesterday?".

"Aye, it's in a paper towel here in my bag".

"Good, can I have it please?"

"Aye of course, wits going on here Donna?".

"We've got no time to explain now girls but we think we've got him".

"Clare, can you get the Hidden Team off Sandra behind the bar please?".

"Sure sure" says Clare.

"Honestly lassies, wit the fuck is going on here?" says Lisa.

"Girls please, just let Donna do what she has to do" says the sensible Babs.

They have the hair and they have the Hidden Team with the finger prints on it. Donna wants all the Factory Girls to stick together and they all walk into the local Police Station. Detective Moriarty is there and listens in to what the girls have to say and takes all the evidence in.

"The hair sample will have to be sent away for analysis ladies but the rest of it makes interesting reading that's for sure" says Detective Moriarty. "We never even knew that these files existed". Great job!!".

"We'll check the finger prints right away but with what you have here ladies, there's definitely enough to bring him in whilst we wait for the DNA sample to come back for sure. If the handwriting on the letters and his report match up, then for sure I'll be able to get a warrant for his arrest on that alone".

All the girls head back to Healy's to Sadie's Snug so Donna and Kirsty can update them all on what they found. It's been a mental 48 hours for the girls, they just hope that they've presented the Police with enough evidence to put the scumbag away for good.

CHAPTER SEVENTEEN

THE TOON IS BACK TO NORMAL

After the high of Teresa's Hen do, the lassies roll into work on the Monday morning full of apprehension about today's events. Will Pedro get arrested or has all of their hard work been in vain and they're miles off the killer still?

Terry comes down from her office with Alan and Jonny and addresses the girls.

"Ok Ladies, I know it's been a mad few weeks around here but let's try and get back to some sort of normality eh? Bonnie's funeral is on Friday so we'll all attend that and shut the Factory for the day shift to attend it".

"Alan and Jonny have kindly volunteered to help with their order as recent events have put us behind so show them what's what and they can help us out this week. I just wanted to thank you all for everything recently. I know it's tough as we've lost not only a colleague, but a friend. Let's hope they catch him soon ladies so Bonnie can rest in peace".

A few of the lassies wipe tears away from their eyes and young Jonny does too. They batter on for a few hours and then they get a couple of visitors to the Factory. Detective

Moriarty and his young partner. Terry halts production and gets everybody on to the shop floor.

"Detective Moriarty has a few words that he'd like to say Ladies & Gentlemen" says Terry.

"Ok, we've got him girls!!" says the Detective.

"Fucking yaaaaaaas" shouts Jan. "Oops sorry, that just slipped out".

"Don't worry Jan haha" says Detective Moriarty. "All of your evidence was spot on Ladies. His fingerprints were on the Hidden Team, his handwriting from the Killing Hall Report matched the letter Mel supposedly sent and most importantly, his DNA is a perfect match from the bodies that we found to the hair on Rose the Hairdresser's floor".

"Everything ties in perfectly and we have him in custody now. The evidence is as clear as day and even if we don't get a confession, we have enough to put him away for good".

"Oh that's absolutely amazing" shouts Debbie.

"Now, I need you all to keep this between us for now Ladies. I've called a Press Conference for outside Healy's at 12.15pm, and I would like you all to stand by my side as I address the Press please?".

"Christ we all better get to Rose's for a blow dry if we're going to be on the telly" jokes Lisa.

"No, I just wanted to come here first and let you all know first before we make it public".

"We wouldn't have caught him as quickly as we have if it wasn't for you girls so thank you each and every single one of you. You've probably saved a few lives into the bargain as well".

The Factory Girls are absolutely buzzing that Pedro has been caught. They're flying through the Gibraltar order and Jonny and Alan are loving all the banter between the lassies on the shop floor as well. The 12 o'clock hooter goes and everybody heads over to Healy's for the big Press Conference.

As everybody walks over the road to Healy's they can see the expectant Press. All the big hitters are there, Jackie Bird & Niall Paterson from Sky. The lassies canny believe it.

"Oh I'm getting a selfie efter this with Jackie Bird" says Donna.

"Aye me tae" says Kirsty.

"Feck Jackie Bird" says Jan. "I want wan wi that Niall from Sky!! Oaft!!"

There's a raised platform outside the bar with about twenty microphones. Detective Moriarty takes the girls into the bar first to brief them up on what's about to happen. They've all to stand to the right hand side of him on the platform and he'll address the awaiting Media.

It's 12.15pm and they all walk out of Healy's to a blinding volley of camera flashes. The girls can hardly see as they make their way up onto the platform. They stand in a line of seven to the right hand side of Detective Moriarty and he approaches the microphone.

"Ladies & Gentlemen and gathered members of the Press. WE'VE GOT HIM!!"

There's a huge roar from everyone, even the Press.

"After a painstaking investigation by ourselves it was actually these seven ladies to my right hand side that presented the evidence to be able to arrest local man "Peter Black". We have concrete evidence and DNA collected from the three deceased ladies that the man we have in custody is the man we've been looking for".

"The full evidence that we have will be presented in Court when that time comes, but I can confirm to you all right now that "Peter Black" has been charged with the murders of local women Marie, Mel and Bonnie and a Report has been sent to the Procurator Fiscal's Office".

"I just wanted to get these ladies up here to give them special thanks and praise. If it wasn't for these local Factory Girls then more poor women may have been murdered so thank you so much ladies".

Everybody starts clapping.

"We'll get to the bottom of why this individual carried out these attacks and also find out if he was working alone. If anybody was in collaboration with this individual then we will bring you to justice as well".

"We won't be taking any questions just now. Many thanks".

Once everybody disperses, Donna and Kirsty run over for a selfie with Jackie Bird and Jan heads for Niall. They all head into Healy's again and JJ bolts the door to keep the Press out.

"Well Girls, how did yous manage it?" says JJ.

"Och we just done a bit of digging JJ" says Kirsty.

"Aye, it was the letter he sent that started us all off".

"I remember in Sammy's shop the other week he told me he bought all the papers to do the crosswords haha. He couldn't even spell crossword the creepy bam".

"He was probably just buying them to read all the reports about himself. That's what Narcissists do" says Babs.

"Well he's behind bars now so hopefully the three lassies can rest in peace now" says Clare.

"It's just weird why he did it. I'm sure it'll all come out in the wash eventually I suppose" says Lisa.

"I wonder if his brother Donald knew about it?" says Debbie.

"Let's not let our minds get ahead of ourselves now Debbie" says Babs. "We need to let the Police interview him and let's see what comes out in the wash".

"Well lassies, we can be proud of ouselves so we can. Let's get back over and get tore right into this Gibraltar order" says Donna.

"Yes ladies, Donna is right" says Terry. "On another note, hopefully this wee toon can get back to normal again now?".

They all head back to the Factory. The killer has been caught but did he work alone? Detective Moriarty has all the evidence he needs to convict Pedro but did he get any help? The town will be waiting with baited breath to see if this is the end of this saga, or is it?

CHAPTER EIGHTEEN

A SURPRISE FOR HUGO

Word has got back to Simon in Spain that everything has settled down now in the town and that the real killer has now been caught. He was chatting to his Mum "Tina" on the phone and is planning a wee surprise trip back to handle what he was meant to the last time.

Tina contacts Russell and gives him Simon's flight details and asks him to keep it hush hush as he has a wee surprise for Hugo when he gets back.

Word gets out in the town that a second arrest has been made following on from Pedro's Murder charge but nobody has a clue who it is yet.

"A pint of lager please Tina" says Hugo.

"Oh ye back on it now son?" says Tina.

"I've been trying tae hide fae Jan for the past fortnight haha".

JJ and Teresa are in the back office.

"Everything is all sorted for the wedding now honey so stop panicking will ye?".

"Oh I was devastated to see all the Irish lot go back after me Hen do JJ, especially me Ma. I'm so homesick JJ".

"Och it'll pass baby. I told you they'd catch the killer here, the town can back to normal now as well. Once we're married and the baby comes, you'll be settled here I promise you".

"Oh I certainly hope so".

Jonny and Alan fly back to Gibraltar on Saturday after their wee visit. Jonny was the last person to be with Bonnie barring her killer so he wants to pay his respects to her on Friday at her funeral.

"I'm gonna miss this place Alan" says Jonny.

"Yes, me too lad. It's been eventful that's for sure".

The plans are in place for Simon's arrival tomorrow and Hugo is about to get the shock of his life too. Tina has informed JJ and Teresa of all the plans and they're absolutely fine with it. Hugo is going to be JJ's best man so he's over the moon for his auld pal.

Meanwhile, back at the Factory.

"Wits Tina invited everybody down to Healy's for at 12.30pm tomorrow for?" asks Debbie.

"Christ knows" says Kirsty but knowing Tina it'll be something good.

"We're hardly getting our fucking lunch breaks these days with all these announcements haha" says Jan.

"Och I canny wait for it" says Donna. "We've no had much good news about here recently so it'll be a wee lift for the toon hopefully".

The big day arrives, it's the day before Bonnie's funeral so Tina wants to give the town and especially Hugo, a bit of amazing news. Simon arrives and is ushered through the back door of Healy's and then everybody starts to arrive at Tina's request of 12.30pm.

One person that everybody is surprised to see in the bar is Donald but after reassurances from everybody, it wasn't him that carried out the murders, it was his brother, so he's given a decent welcome by everyone.

Everybody is in and JJ bolts the door of the pub. Tina stands on a chair at the end of the bar.

"Right folks, listen in!!" shouts Tina.

The pub falls silent.

"Ok, it's been a shite time for most of us in this town recently but hopefully we'll all be able to put that behind us soon. I've got a massive surprise for one of you in here today and it's for you Hugo".

Hugo looks up from his pint in utter disbelief.

"Kmeer son" says Tina.

Hugo walks over to Tina and stands beside her.

"Right, not a lot of people know this but see this guy here, he would do anything for anybody and give you his last penny. He's a great guy and had a really tough life but he'd rather still help others than himself".

"I've got some people here who want to say hello and then we have an even bigger surprise for you at the end as our way of saying thank you".

"First of all, my son Simon went through an awful time after his marriage to the recently departed Marie went tits up after 16 years. This guy here took the reins and and helped my son move to Spain and now he's set for life, so my first surprise for you is my son Simon. Out you come son".

Simon walks out the back office and Hugo canny believe it. He gives Simon a big hug and Tina steps down from the chair and Simon steps up.

"Hiya folks, thanks to my Mum for that introduction and thanks to Hugo for everything. We've brought you here today because we haven't finished yet. When Hugo lived out on the Costa Del Sol in the 1990's, he changed so many people's lives for the better. One of them was a man named Bruno".

"NO!!!" shouts Hugo.

"Now Hugo took this young man under his wing out there. Bruno was nothing but a petty criminal and a thug and Hugo turned this young man's life completely around. He's now a wealthy businessman and entrepreneur. Come on out Bruno!!"

Bruno makes his way out of the office and into the bar. Hugo genuinely can't believe this. Again he hugs his old pal for what seems an eternity. Everybody is clapping and cheering. Bruno replaces Simon on the chair.

"Aw fur fuck sake, wit now?" shouts Hugo.

"So Ladies and Gentleman, Hugo not only changed my life but he changed others too. A gentleman named Mustapha from Morrocco as well".

"Jesus suffering fuck no" shouts Hugo.

"Wait Hugo, wait" laughs Bruno. Mustapha was like me, a career criminal but he's now built schools, villages and wells in poor Morroccan towns thanks to Hugo and is a succesful and crime free individual now thanks to this man here. Out you come Mustapha".

"This is fucking unreal man!!" screams Hugo.

Mustapha comes up, they embrace and then he replaces Bruno on the chair.

"Aw wit noo?" says Hugo.

"This is like an episode of "This is Your Life" whispers Jan to Lisa.

"There's nobody in here barring the three or four of us that know about this but I'm sure Hugo wont mind me telling this story with what's about to happen in the next half an hour or so. On one of his visits to Morrocco to see me, Hugo brought his beautiful woman "Siham" with him on one of his trips. He was with his friend Donald who's standing over there and he brought his beautiful lady "Helima".

"On that fateful trip, unfortunately Hugo's good lady "Siham" died from choking on her vomit in the Hotel that they were staying in. She was sharing a bed with Helima as the lads were out partying. I know Hugo was never the same after that night but I have one more guest for you Hugo".

The door opens and out walks this beautiful woman in her late 40's. It's Helima. Hugo puts both his hands over his mouth and is absolutely stunned. Donald can't quite believe his eyes either. They embrace and both of them burst out crying. She then walks over to Donald and embraces him also. The punters in the bar are just stunned. Helima replaces Mustapha on the chair.

"Please excuse my English as it isn't perfect please. My beautiful friend "Siham" and myself were introduced to Hugo and Donald in the 1990's. Both of them were brilliant for us. Although myself and Donald had a great time, Siham and Hugo fell madly in love with each other. Siham unfortunately died or I'm sure she and Hugo would still be together to this very day".

"Hugo changed my life massively as well. The money that he left us got my children a First Class education and they are now very successful in their fields thanks to him. I still visit "Siham" daily and I know she is with you Hugo. One thing that I've heard is that you and Donald are not friends anymore and this disappoints me".

"Donald, a lot of bad happens in this world but so does a lot of good. It's not Hugo's fault that we split, it was my choice. You had your life and I had mine there. Please make up with him for me. Hugo, we have one final surprise for you but we need to go a little walk from here".

Simon gets everyone together. Helima takes Hugo's hand on her right hand side and Donald's on her left and they walk towards the shore front.

"Promise me you two will make up from this day forward Donald" says Helima.

"I promise you Helima we will" says Donald.

They all break hands and Hugo and Donald shake on it.

They arrive at this big shiny new building and Simon stands on the stairs leading up to it to address the crowd.

"As you heard in the pub folks, this guy means so much to so many different people so we've all clubbed together and done something for him for a change. Hugo had his own place out on the Costa Del Sol in the 1990's named "Hugo's" and it's exact dimensions are now here behind me on this shore front".

Bruno, Helima and Mustapha are now on the roof terrace of the building where there's a white sheet covering the sign.

"So, Bruno, Mustapha and Helima, if you'd like to do the honours please?".

They remove the white sheet covering the sign and pull it up to the roof terrace.

"SIHAM's"

"Welcome to Siham's everybody!!" says Simon.

"Now she will always be with you everyday Hugo" shouts Helima from the roof terrace.

"It's all yours pal" say Simon.

Simon throws Hugo the keys and he is absolutely gobsmacked.

Hugo gets the guided tour of his new establishment. Not that he needs it. It's exactly the same dimensions as his old bar "Hugo's" in La Linea back in the 1990's. Mustapha and Bruno come downstairs to have a drink with everyone and Helima takes Hugo up to the roof terrace alone, arm in arm. They take in the beautiful views of the Isle of Arran & Ailsa Craig.

"Hugo, this is what Siham would've wanted for you. I still talk with her spirit every day and I just know she'd want this for you. You were everything for her and now she can be with you every single day now".

Hugo starts crying.

"I fucking miss her Helima. Every single day but this will help me keep her spirit alive. I knew after what happened, I couldn't ever go back and visit her and it tore me apart every single day but now I can visit her daily now. Thank you from the bottom of my heart".

"No thank you, you have no idea how many people's lives that you've changed".

Tomorrow is Bonnie's funeral. Hopefully the last of bad days for this wee town.

At least for a while....

CHAPTER NINETEEN

REST IN PEACE BONNIE

It's Friday morning, the day of Bonnie's funeral and the day shift Factory Girls have been given the day off to attend it. The plan is to meet in Healy's at 10am and then walk down to the Chapel for the funeral at 11am. It's bound to be packed as Bonnie was very popular in the town.

Alan and Jonny are getting ready for it at the B&B.

"You ok son?" asks Alan.

"Not really Alan, I should've walked her home or got her a taxi".

"Jonny, listen to the people around here, she was a free spirit. She probably would've walked back in the end anyway regardless of what you said. She probably walked along the beach to feel the edge of the water through her toes on the sand as the sun was rising. It's not your fault that monster did what he did. Don't beat yourself up about it kid".

"I know you're right Alan, I just keep thinking, what if?".

"Well don't kiddo right. What's done is done, let's go and give her a good send off lad. This is our last day here, let's enjoy it pal".

"You're right old pal, let's just do that".

Word has got round the town that the second person arrested for Bonnie's murder is none other than a Mr Longshanks and the town is stunned.

Kirsty is getting ready at Donna's.

"No way can it be Longshanks surely Donna?"

"Well they've no arrested him for nothing huv they?"

"Aye true but I canny see that auld duffer killing anybody".

"Ye never know Kirsty, ye never know".

JJ opens the Bar at 9.30am and lets Teresa have a long lie in. Alberto is already in sorting out the buffet for the wake afterwards. Sandra offers to cover the bar whilst everybody attends the funeral.

"That's amazing what everybody did for Hugo yesterday eh JJ?" says Sandra.

"Yes it is, he is one special guy".

"Why did you pick him to be your best man?"

"It was easy really, he's been my best pal since I was a wee boy really, even though he's much older. He's always been there for me and continues to be. The guy is one in a million so I couldn't think of anyone better, plus his patter will be on the ball for the speech hopefully".

"Did ye hear aboot Longshanks as well JJ?"

"Aye, mental that. Let's see what comes of that. Knowing him, he'll wriggle his way out of it".

Everyone starts to filter in to Healy's and Longshanks is the talk of the place.

"It would be brilliant to see that bastard finally go down for everything he's done over the years" says Colin.

"Aye bro, he was a bastard to us in that Slaughterhoose all those years ago eh?" says John.

Hugo walks in as proud as punch with his visitors Helima, Bruno, Simon and Mustapha. Simon is gonna stay back with the visitors in Healy's as they never knew Bonnie.

"I wish Pepe & Jesus were here to see Siham's place too" says Hugo.

"What happened to those two Bruno?" asks Helima.

"Jesus died about ten years ago in a Road Traffic Accident just outside Estepona and Pepe died last year of Cancer".

"Ah God rest them" says Mustapha.

Alan and Jonny walk in next.

"Remember what I told you back at the B&B son?"

"Yes Alan, I won't let you or Bonnie down today old pal, let's enjoy it".

The Factory Girls are all in the Snug.

"What songs did Bonnie pick Terry?" asks Clare.

"She only picked one, we know she was a bit of a hippy pot head so no surprise really". "Redemption Song" by Bob Marley was what she wanted to go out with".

"Ah, great choice that" says Lisa.

"Wits up with your coupon Jan? ask Debbie.

"I'm just gutted about Hugo's day yesterday. I thought that I might've stood a chance with him but after hearing his love story yesterday, his heart is definitely elsewhere".

"Oh don't worry darling, there's somebody for all of us" says Babs. "Yous had a good time a few weeks ago so just hold on to that memory".

"Aye a suppose you're right Babs" says Jan.

After some Coffee, Tea and breakfast rolls that Alberto done for everybody, the punters from the pub head down to the Chapel for Bonnie's service. After forty five minutes of lovely stories about her, the entourage head to the local cemetery to bury her.

After the cemetery, everybody heads back to Healy's were Alberto once more, has put on a beautiful spread for everybody to enjoy. Bonnie's family requested a disco and a karaoke for her in Healy's as she'd want everyone to enjoy themselves. Old Jimmy already has all the equipment set up for everyone coming back.

"What is this here with the microphone Hugo my friend?" asks Mustapha.

"It's called Karaoke my old pal. You'll enjoy it, people get up and sing their favourite songs with the words on the screen".

"What will you sing Hugo?" giggles Helima.

"I'll put your name up to sing if there's any more of your carry on Missy".

"Hugo it's great seeing you again my old friend" says Bruno. "Everybody back home still asks about you, we must get a group photo. Nobody will believe I'm back with the legend".

"Oh I'm no legend Bruno, I'm just a quiet guy getting on with life".

"Hugo you are a legend mate" says Simon. "Myself and Bruno are booked on the same flight as Alan and Jonny tomorrow by all accounts, so Russell is going to take us all to the airport. We'll introduce ourselves to them later. Helima and Mustapha go back on Sunday so you have an extra day with them".

"Cool mate, no bother" says Hugo.

Donna & Kirsty are first up on the Karaoke and they're murdering "Girls Just Wanna Have Fun". The place is heaving and everybody is tucking into the buffet. Alberto even did a side Morroccan buffet for the town's new visitors which was much appreciated by them.

Alan pulls young Jonny to the one side.

"Well young man, how are you feeling now?" says Alan.

"Do you know what old pal. Your advice was spot on today. Let's enjoy the rest of the night and give her a great send off".

Both of the guys raise their glasses.

"Rest in Peace Bonnie!!" shouts young Jonny.

CHAPTER TWENTY

BYE, BYE, LONGSHANKS

Now this town has had it's fair share of bastard's over the years. Most recently would obviously be Pedro Black after what he did to those three women. I think over a fifty to seventy year span though of being a complete arsehole, the title would go to Mr Longshanks who's brought nothing but misery to the people of this town.

The whole town woke up to the tremendous news this morning that Mr Longshanks has been charged with "Conspiracy to Murder" following the death of Mel from the pub but not the other two women where the charges have been dropped. Detective Moriarty goes to Terry's house to explain.

"Come in Detective" says Terry. "Can I get you a cuppa there?".

"No thanks Terry, this shouldn't take long. Ok, so we've proven beyond reasonable doubt that Mr Longshanks was behind "Peter Black" murdering Mel from the Bar. We have the text messages between them both and Longshanks was behind it all. His motive was to try and get the Textile's Factory shut down so he could knock it down still and build luxury flats".

"Oh my god!!" says Terry.

"He hired Peter to pick anyone at random and dump their body in the Factory building they both knew so well. Mel was locking the pub up and Peter knew she'd be there alone in the dark so struck. It seems that Pedro just got his lust for blood after that so carried on. The other two were nothing to do with Longshanks".

"Apparently Pedro tried it on with Marie as nobody else would go near her and she knocked him back. This infuriated Pedro so she had to go. Bonnie was her best pal so she was the natural choice to be next. It's all came out in the wash through interrogation and will be regurgitated in the High Court soon".

"So what will happen to Longshanks then?" asks Terry.

"Conspiracy to Murder is the same as doing the murder yourself. If proven guilty, which he will be with the evidence we have against him, he won't see the light of day again at his age. He will die in prison. Bye, bye, Longshanks".

"Oh wow, the town will be ecstatic at that news" says Terry.

"Well to be honest Terry and this is between us".

"Of course Detective".

"After reading the Inspector's reports from the Slaughterhouse he owned, I hope somebody does to him and to Pedro in Prison, what they let happen to those poor pigs and women. The stuff myself and my team have had to sit and read through plus the grim discoveries we've had to witness, they both deserve what they get".

"Indeed Detective".

"Ok Terry, I just thought I'd let you know the news and I'm sure I can trust you to let Teresa & JJ know too as the charge only really affects Mel and I'm sure they'd want to know".

"Yes, I'll let them know right away Detective cheers".

"Have a nice day Terry".

Terry immediately jumps in her car and heads to Healy's to let JJ and Teresa know the news. Simon, Bruno, Hugo, Helima, Mustapha, Alan & Jonny are already in the bar awaiting Russell to take the four boys to the airport.

Hugo pulls Jonny to the one side.

"Listen son, we got off on the wrong foot here and it's my fault. I don't want you leaving here thinking bad of me now".

"Ah it's fine Hugo, it was my fault. You have all been so kind to us since we've been here. I was apprehensive about coming here as my Dad was a Bank Manager and his bank got robbed by two Scotsmen but thankfully they are both dead now. Davie and Kris Little? Have you heard of them Hugo?.

"Erm no son, their names don't ring a bell. Anyway, here's a wee wedge of money, you get yersel and my auld pal Alan a few pints at the airport son ok".

"Yes ok Hugo, cheers".

Jonny walks away and Bruno and Simon walk over to Hugo.

"Hugo my friend, thank you once again for everything" says Bruno. "I know you can't visit us but we'll certainly visit you more often now that you have Siham's".

"I'd really like that Bruno old pal".

"I concur with Bruno mate, wild horses couldn't drag me away from Spain now but that place round the corner is special man. Thanks for everything you did for me after my marriage breakup once more old pal".

"Isn't that what pals do?"

Russell's taxi arrives and they all say their goodbyes. Alan is last up and he gives Hugo a hug.

"Cheers old pal Hugo" says Alan. "Remember one thing Hugo, you'll always be a good cunt to me".

"Haha. Cheers auld yin and safe journey".

Rose turns up to give Simon a hug at the taxi, she's devastated he's away again but understands he has to go. Tina gives him his last hug and then Russell's Taxi departs for the airport. Tina, Rose, Hugo, Helima and Mustapha stand outside Healy's and wave them off.

Terry walks in to JJ's office to let him and Teresa know the good news. She explains everything that Detective Moriarty did and JJ is over the moon.

"Fuck him the old bastard, he deserves everything that's coming to him after what he's did to this town, it's Karma".

"JJ, language" says Teresa.

"Och nae wonder, he's been horrible to everybody here all his life Teresa".

"JJ's right here Teresa, he deserves it all".

The pub starts to fill up for Saturday night disco night. Siham's has it's Grand Opening next Saturday so Hugo decides to treat Helima and Mustapha to their last night in Healy's. Helima and Mustapha have never seen anything like this before and Hugo is loving it watching them both letting their hair down.

The Factory Girls arrive and they get a big cheer from everybody as they walk in. They're celebrities in this toon now after putting Pedro behind bars and subsequently Longshanks as well. They won't have to buy a drink in this town again.

CHAPTER TWENTY ONE

NEW BEGINNINGS

It's been a bit of a lonely few weeks for Donald. He noticed that his brother had been distancing himself from him over the past few months but he never knew why and now he does. People in the town are giving him funny looks as well just because he's Pedro's brother. He's taking a walk along the shore front before heading to the bookies to put his Sunday fitba coupon on just thinking about life and his own future.

Colin & John are already in the bookies and they're giving Tam behind the counter it stinking already.

"Hawl Tam!!" shouts Colin.

"Wit?" says Tam.

"Why should you never be rude to a jumps jockey?"

"I don't know Colin, why"?

"In case he takes offence" (A Fence) "Get it Tam haha?"

"Aww piss aff you!!" says Tam.

The lads have been doing well recently with their accumulators and are hoping to empty Tam's till again today.

In walks Hugo.

"Morning Thomas, Colin, John!!"

"Morning Hugo!!"

"I'm just in for a quick hawf an hour boys, my Morroccan visitors are leaving today. Phoenix Taxi's are picking them up at midday".

"Hey that bird Helima is a big darling Hugo" says John.

"Aye she is that mate, a lovely woman".

"How did Donald manage to pump that fur fuck sake?" says Colin.

Just at that, Donald walks into the bookies.

"Ah, speak of the Devil!!" shouts Colin.

"Donald!!" shouts Hugo. "Mon in pal".

"Pal?" says Tam. "That you two finally made up now?".

"Aye Tam, life is too short mate".

"Morning boys, what's the tips the day?" says Donald.

"Still looking Donald, still looking" says John.

Hugo motions Donald over to the other side of the bookies for a chat.

"What's up with your coupon these days?" says Hugo.

"Och just everything Hugo. With what's happened with Pedro, the way folk round here are looking at me, and Helima leaving again today. I just feel like life is kicking me right in the baws at the minute".

"Right you, fucking listen to me right. What your brother did has fuck all to do with you ok. Never mind the folk round here, I'll no be long in sorting that out and Helima, again, you know the score there mate. Listen, we're pals again, come and work for me at Siham's mate. Back to the good old days eh?".

"Really?"

"Yes really. I need a Manager, somebody I can trust and even though we've had our differences over the years, you've always had my back. Especially over in Spain and you done the main thing all these years. Kept your mouth shut!! The bar opens officially on Saturday, come round on Friday at 5pm and meet your staff. The job is yours old pal".

"I don't know what to say Hugo".

"New beginnings Donald, new beginnings. See you Friday!!".

Donald's whole demeanour changes and he's actually smiling again. He now has something to live for. Hugo heads back to his place to get Mustapha and Helima as Russell will be collecting them for the airport in an hour or so.

Tony is another wee lost soul in the town. After getting barred from Healy's he's had to drink in the downmarket bar at the other end of town, "The Mermaid". He misses the craic with everybody, especially his brother's Colin and John. He walks into Sammy's for the Sunday papers.

"Morning Sammy"

"Ah, morning Tony. Wit ye efter pal?"

"Och just the Sunday papers".

"Nae bother".

JJ walks in to get the Sunday papers in for Healy's.

"Morning Sammy, Tony".

"Morning JJ" says both.

It's a little bit awkward as Tony and JJ are stood beside the papers. Like a Mexican standoff.

"Eh JJ?"

"Yes Tony".

"Listen mate, I want to apologise for that day of Marie's wake when I was a total fanny of a guy". "I've already seen her faither and apologised too".

"Well that's big of you Tony".

"Listen JJ, will you give me one more chance mate? I promise I'll hold my tongue from now on".

"Tony, we've all been there mate but you were bang out of order that day. Your feelings probably were the same as a lot of the locals but you stupidly blurted it out. If you've apologised to her Da and now you've apologised to me, then I'm happy with that pal. I'm happy to give you another chance Tony. We draw a line in the sand today and start again ok?".

"Ok man, cheers!!"

"No bother Tony, new beginnings pal. I'll let the staff know".

JJ heads back to Healy's and lets everyone know that Tony's barring has been lifted and Tony heads to the bookies to let his brother's know the good news.

Back at Healy's, Teresa is having a heart to heart with Tina & Sandra before opening up.

"Ladies can I ask your advice please and this goes no further?" says Teresa.

"Of course hen" says Tina.

"I want to go home to Ireland and I don't know how to break it to JJ".

"What!! Now?" says Sandra.

"No no Sandra, after the wedding and the babby coming. I've been hinting to JJ but he's having none of it".

"You have to do what's right for you and your wean hen" says Tina.

"I just miss me mammy and I think it'll only get worse when babby comes".

"Why don't you speak to Terry about it Teresa, she knows JJ better than anyone" says Sandra. "Maybe she can talk him round?".

"What about Healy's though Teresa?" says Tina.

"Oh I know, I love the pub and I love the people that drink in it, it's just not home" says Teresa.

"It's a tough one darling it really is but you have to do what's best for the three of yous once you put that ring on your finger" says Sandra.

"I'm just thinking about going home and being around my family and I can't get it out of my head, new beginnings".

Just at that, JJ walks into the pub with the Sunday papers.

"Ah ladies, the very people. I've lifted Tony's barring so he's free to come back into the pub but he knows now that he's on his final warning in here".

"Wit?" says Sandra.

"Och, new beginnings and all that ladies".

JJ puts the papers on the bar and heads through to the office.

"Thanks girls, I think I'll speak to Terry".

Hugo gets home to Mustapha and Helima all packed and good to go.

"All sorted guys?" says Hugo.

"Yes we are Hugo, thank you for putting us up" says Mustapha. I'm just going to take a quick walk along the shore to Siham's and give it one last look, I'll be back in time for the taxi don't worry".

Mustapha departs and goes for a wee walk.

"Hugo, I was jealous of you and Siham back in the day. She was so in love with you and I hoped to find that connection with someone one day but haven't yet. I'm so happy she'll now be with you every single day. I have a gift for you before I go".

"Helima you've done enough".

Helima reaches into her suitcase and pulls out a golden frame. It's a framed photo of Siham. Hugo notices her face and breaks down crying.

"Mustapha knew what I was going to give you Hugo so he went for a walk so that you can get your emotions out. I knew the one thing you didn't have was a photo of her, you can proudly hang this in Siham's now. I also have one last gift".

"Helima, that's more than enough".

She reaches into her suitcase once more and produces a small white envelope.

"What's this Helima?"

"Open it Hugo!!"

Hugo carefully opens it and it's a lock of jet black hair.

"What? Who's?

"It's Siham's lock of hair Hugo. When we were preparing her body in Morrocco, I cut a lock of her hair off when you were washing her body and meant to give it to you then but forgot. I've kept it all of these years but it belongs to you".

"I'm just stunned Helima, absolutely stunned here".

A few minutes pass and Mustapha arrives back. He gives Hugo one final hug. Hugo then embraces Helima and there's a toot from a horn outside. Russell has arrived to take them to the airport.

"We both love you very dearly Hugo and we promise we'll be back to see you" says Helima.

"Goodbye my friend" says Mustapha.

The taxi drives away and Hugo walks back into his house. He sits for what seems like hours, just staring at Siham's picture.

CHAPTER TWENTY TWO

ORDER COMPLETE

It's two weekends until Teresa & JJ's big day and on Saturday, Siham's is open for business. JJ and Teresa have agreed to switch their reception at the last minute from Healy's to the stunning new Siham's and have informed all the guests. It's JJ's best man gift to Hugo and it will give his new business an excellent start.

Meanwhile back at the Factory, the girls are on the final straight with the huge Gibraltar order. They're a week behind with the Police closing the Factory due to finding Mel's body in the abandoned store-room.

"Right ladies, this is the final stretch with this order, let's smash it out and enjoy Saturday night at Siham's".

"Yer fucking rooting tooting Terry" shouts Jan.

The lassies power on with the order and the craic is flowing too.

"I don't fucking believe it lassies" says Donna. "I drove up tae my hoose last night and I noticed something different. I thought, wit is it? Some wee black bastards have stolen my purple hanging baskets. Dae ye believe that?".

"Och yer kidding?" says Kirsty.

"Naw I'm no kidding. I had a wee special ornament in them and everything. I'm gonnae drive aboot the toon later and see if I can see them".

"Och darling that's terrible" says Babs.

"I know Babs, I liked to water them and everything" says Donna.

Talk turns to the new establishment in town.

"Some place that new Siham's eh?" says Kirsty.

"Aye, I canny wait to get on that roof terrace at night wi a wee glass of Champers and take in those views" says Clare.

"Ah that sounds lovely that Clare" says Babs.

"I canny wait till Hugo takes me up there and gets a view eh my arse whilst I'm taking in they views haha" shouts Jan.

"Jaaaaaaaaaaaaaaaan" laughs Debbie.

"I call it how I see it girls, you know me" Jan says.

"Oh a wee glass of Champagne on that terrace Clare, we're defo doing that Saturday pal" says Lisa.

"Lassies, Clare is right. Do you know what? We should be fucking proud of ourselves these past few months. We should all get on that roof with a glass of Champagne and toast "The Factory Girls" because not only did we catch a Serial Killer, we've worked our arses aff in here and deserve it".

"Here fucking here!!" shouts Jan.

Teresa walks into the Factory and goes straight up to Terry's office and knocks on the door.

"Terry, can I have a word please?"

"Of course you can honey, come in and close the door. What can I do for you Teresa?".

"I don't know how to break this to you Terry. Oh, I'll just come out with it. I want to go home to Ireland".

"What? Now? Surely not!!"

"No no Terry, not right now. Once the wedding and the babby is done. I was chatting with Tina and Sandra about it and they suggested I speak with you for advice. I've been trying to hint to JJ about it for months now but he's just brushing it off and is blaming my hormones".

"Darling, I know he's my son but he might just be right you know. We do silly things when we're pregnant like eat stuff we'd never ever normally eat and make rash decisions".

"I miss me Mammy too Terry, I know you're me Mammy over here but you know what I mean? I think I'll miss her more when I have the babby too. I'm scared Terry to tell you the truth".

"Oh honey, listen to me. You're not the first woman in the world and you certainly won't be the last to feel the way you do right now, it's all very natural believe me. Your Mammy is less than an hour away on a flight and you have your new big family here, this whole town. You'll feel completely different when the baby comes, trust me, because all of your thoughts will be on that precious little thing".

"Thanks for the chat Terry, I really need to think about everything but you've made me think that little bit clearer now and put me at ease so thank you. Please don't say anything to JJ".

"I won't honey I promise. Wait!! I have an idea that might help you guys and me too".

"What Terry?"

"Why don't you come here and work with me?"

"Sorry?"

"I haven't replaced Bonnie yet and you're good with computers and numbers. You're under each others feet over there and at home 24/7. Once you've had the baby and you're ready, come and work here at the Factory".

"Do you know what Terry, that doesn't sound like such a bad idea, let me think about that".

Teresa wipes the tears away from her eyes and Terry hands her some baby wipes to clean her face. Teresa leaves the Factory and heads back to Healy's.

Tina is behind the bar and it's only Donald that's in at the minute.

"Quiet in here the day Tina" says Donald.

"Aye, so far Donald. Folk don't have the money fur it anymore pal".

"Aye true Tina".

"You're missed oor at the bookies, it's no the same oor there anymore either".

"Auld Tam still penny pinching haha?".

"Aye, every penny is a prisoner wi him. I think Colin and John have been giving him a battering recently".

Teresa sees that there's people in the bar now so slips in the back door in case they can see that she's been crying.

"Speak of the devil Donald, looks who's just walked in? Colin, John, Tony!! How are ye boys?

"Good Tina, three pints a lager please" says Colin.

"Good to see you back Tony" says Tina.

"Cheers. I'll try and keep my comments to masel this time haha".

Tina pours the three pints and gives them to the boys. It's nearing lunch time so the Factory Girls will be in soon. The door opens and in walks Rose.

"Oh hiya Rose" says Donald. "Looking very glam as usual".

"Oh cheers Donald" says Rose.

The three brothers are all watching her wiggle as she walks to the end of the bar.

"I'll have a wee glass of White Wine please Tina" says Rose.

"No bother hen, no busy the day?".

"Och naw it's quiet so I thought I'd pop in for a wee Vino pal. How's your Simon getting on?"

"Och he's fine Rose, have you still got a wee thing for him?"

"I'll always have a wee thing for him, I'll just wait until he's ready".

"Och bless ya" says Tina.

In walk the Factory Girls and head towards Sadie's Snug.

"Come and sit wi us Rose" shouts Babs.

"Aye nae bother lassies".

Rose heads over to the snug whilst Jan and Kirsty head to the bar for the round.

"The normal for our table please Tina" says Kirsty.

"Good to see you back Tony" says Jan. "I think I was next in line to get barred fae here but that's me back doon to second place now haha".

"Aye cheers Jan" says Tony.

The lassies take the drinks over to the snug.

"So Rose, are you looking forward to the big wedding?".

"Aye lassies. A 7am start for me that day, I've got all of yous to do before it all starts at 2pm. I'm all excited for it".

"It should be some day that's for sure with all the mad Irish in town. I'm hearing that Cormac is some boy" says Babs.

"Did I tell ye about my purple hanging baskets Rose?" says Donna.

JJ comes out of the toilet and walks back into the office to see Teresa fixing her face.

"Are you ok baby? Have you been crying?".

"No no JJ, just sorting me make up out, it was a bit skew whiff that's all".

The lassies head back over to the Factory after their lunch and over the next few days complete the big Gibraltar order. Order complete!! Friday night in Healy's is a quiet one because the big one is tomorrow night with the Grand Opening of the very swish Siham's.

CHAPTER TWENTY THREE

SIHAM'S

It's exactly one week until the hottest wedding of the year. The fact now that the reception is going to be in Siham's, it gives everyone, especially JJ & Teresa, the perfect opportunity to try out the trendy new hotspot in town. It's "invite only" tonight and Hugo has invited 100 VIP guests.

Hugo asked JJ if he could hire Alberto for tonight and for the wedding reception also and of course JJ agreed. Alberto has put on a lovely spread for the invited guests tonight and Donald is stood at the front door as the new Manager in his Tuxedo, welcoming in all the guests.

As soon as you walk into Siham's, there's a stunning gold framed picture of the lady herself and Hugo is in his Tuxedo stood proudly beside her. Teresa & JJ are the first to arrive.

"Wow, Donald, Hugo, look at you two!!" says Teresa. "Swoot swoo boys".

"Same to yourself Teresa, looking swell" says Hugo.

"Is that Siham in that picture Hugo?" says JJ.

"It certainly is mate".

"Wow man, she was sensational Hugo, you were one lucky man brother".

"I was indeed JJ".

"What a place to have our reception in JJ, the place is absolutely stunning" says Teresa.

"It certainly is Princess".

Hugo has put on a free glass of Champagne for guests on arrival and encourages them to take in the views of the roof terrace.

"Would you look at those views JJ" says Teresa.

"I know beautiful. That's Ailsa Craig there on the left hand side, that little Rock. Straight ahead, that's the Isle of Arran".

"Ah, it's beautiful sure" says Teresa.

Teresa looks into JJ's eyes and gives him a kiss.

The place starts to fill up and it's not long before the Factory Girls are on the roof terrace.

"Ok Ladies, I'd like to propose the first toast of the evening if yous don't mind" says Terry.

"Of course not boss" says Debbie.

"We lost one of our colleagues recently. Not only was she our colleague but she was a friend to us all too. She was found just over there on that beach and she should be with us tonight. In fact, she is with us tonight. To Bonnie!!".

"To Bonnie!!" says all.

"I'd like to propose a toast too lassies" says Donna. "We spoke about this the other day in the Factory and we fucking deserve this tonight. Terry just mentioned Bonnie, well we got Bonnie the justice she deserved by nailing her killer. We did it lassies, us!! We've worked hard to get that Gibraltar order out even when Longshanks tried to shut us down again. Us!! So, regardless of what happens from now on in, we've proven that as long as us Factory Girls stick together, we can take on the World. To The Factory Girls!!".

"The Factory Girls!!"

Jan makes a bee-line for Hugo.

"Hugo, look, I'm not chasing you tonight ok. I just want to say you look amazing in you Tux pal".

"Aw thanks Jan, I appreciate that, I really do".

"The picture as you walk in, is that Siham?.

"It is aye".

"My God, she is absolutely stunning Hugo. No wonder you wanted to marry her".

"She was definitely one of a kind Jan, just like you pal haha".

Everybody is having a great wee night and the place looks sensational. Hugo is getting nervous as it's nearly time for his big speech but it'll be practice for him for the wedding next Saturday. Donald takes to the microphone first.

"Ladies and Gentlemen, if everybody could make their way outside please as we're about to do the official opening of Siham's".

Everybody starts to filter outside and down the steps to the well lit area outside the stunning front door. Donald passes the microphone to Hugo and pulls the red ribbon across the front door and holds the scissors until Hugo has finished his speech. Hugo puts the Mic to his mouth.

"Ladies and Gentlemen. First of all, I'll try my best not to swear here ok so bear with me on that one. I'm probably as shocked to be stood here tonight as all of you are to be honest. I have seen the guys building this up as I went on my daily stroll along the shore before I went to the bookies and to think that when it was complete, that I'd own it, well, let me tell you, it's completely blown me away".

Now, to the name of it, Siham's. There's only one person here that ever met Siham and it was that man stood there, Donald. He's stood by my side today and he was by my side the day she died too. Now I want to put this to bed right now and it's maybe not the time or the place but you all know me. What that man's brother did has absoloutely nothing to do with him so don't tar that man with the same brush as his brother.

Everybody starts clapping their hands.

"Well said Hugo" shouts Tony.

"Now back to Siham. You all know me in this town as this big roughty toughty aggressive guy and that's what you see, but in all honesty it couldn't be further from the truth. When I met Siham, my life completely changed. I met a young, beautiful, compassionate, kind and loving person and she was absolutely perfect for me in every way, shape and form. She's stood behind me right now and probably blushing at what I'm saying but it's all true".

"Something changed in me the day I met her and something died in me the day that she died. It's only recently that I've managed to finally realise that's she's gone. Something again that only Donald knows about. I prepared her body for burial, an Islamic burial. It opened my eyes and it was a beautiful day that I'll never forget. I can still see her perfect face now. I'll leave you with this".

"Her friend Helima visited us recently and she gave me a lock of Siham's hair from that day we prepared her body. Also I didn't have a photo of her either, hence the big one there in the hallway that she gave me too. The hardest thing for me after losing Siham was that I never had a place to go and visit her and now I do, we all do. Welcome to "Siham's" Ladies and Gentlemen!!".

Hugo gets a huge round of applause. Donald passes him the scissors and Hugo cuts the ribbon. Most of the women are crying and Donald wipes a tear from his eye too.

"What a lovely speech that was Hugo" says Donald.

"Thanks pal, I didn't have a clue what I was gonna say, it just came oot".

"Well, she'll be proud of you tonight mate that's for sure".

"Thanks pal".

Everybody goes back and enjoys the rest of the night. It's a complete success and Siham's goes down an absolute storm with the locals.

CHAPTER TWENTY FOUR

THE IRISH ARRIVE IN TOWN

It's only two days until the wedding and today, the Irish contingent all arrive. JJ is particularly shitting himself because big Cormac, Mairead and Karen were only told by their mother on her death bed a year ago about the late Father Peter Jackson. The big brother that they never knew about. He's buried in the Town and JJ needs some advice about how to go about getting them to the cemetery to visit him so he pops over to the bookies to see Hugo.

"Oh hiya Paige" says JJ. "Nae Tam today?".

"No, he's been off sick for a few days now JJ".

"Did somebody win a lot of money haha? Hugo, Donald, Colin, John, how's it going boys?".

"Aye no bad JJ" says all.

"Hugo can I talk to you quickly mate?"

"Course pal, course".

"I'm fucking bricking it the day man. All the Irish lot are coming over. Russell is dropping them off about 1pm and they only found out about Father Peter Jackson about a year ago and haven't been to his grave yet. How do I play this man?".

"Once they're settled, take them down to his grave mate. Kids out of wedlock especially in Ireland in a Catholic family was frowned upon big time back then, it's changed days now JJ, they'll completely understand".

"Aye you're right Hugo, that's wit al day. Yer speech sorted for Saturday yet?".

"Och, I'll jist wing it like I did the other night at Siham's haha".

"Some guy Hugo, right pal, I better get back oor the road".

JJ fires across the road to Healy's and his mum is in the back office with Teresa The pub will be empty today because Pedro Black and Mr Longshanks are getting sentenced today at the High Court in Glasgow and most of the punters are away up to see what they get.

"Where have you been JJ" asks Teresa.

"Och I was just oor seeing Hugo quickly at the bookies".

"Ye canny leave this lassie alone now JJ. It's only four weeks until she goes now, she could go at any minute ye know".

"Aye Mum, aye".

One o'clock approaches and JJ is getting more and more nervous and then the beep of the horn comes. Phoenix Taxi's Minibus is outside. Terry, Teresa and JJ go outside to greet them all. Russell opens the side door and they all pile out one by one. Teresa is beaming.

"Awwww Mum, Bernadette, Dougal, Frances, Margaret, Aunty Karen, Conor, Tim, Niall, Sean, Aiden and Uncle Cormac!! How are ye all?" says Teresa.

Aiden goes straight for JJ, they were best pals when he was over in Ballincollig.

"JJ the legend, how are ye ya langer?" says Aiden.

"Aw Aiden, great to see you pal".

JJ has been nervous about the Father Peter Jackson thing and in particular was hoping to avoid the massive Cormac but no such luck. His big shovel like hawns crash onto JJ's shoulder.

"JJ my boy, how are ye?".

"Ermm fine Cormac, I'm ermm hoping you're alright too".

"I'm fine my boy, my favourite niece is getting married to my favourite Scotsman. What kind of Whiskys do you have my boy, I want to sample the lot of them".

"Eh, fill yer boots Cormac".

"Tina, eh, give Cormac our finest Whisky pal and make it a double".

"Coming right up JJ" says Tina.

They chew the fat for the next hour or so and Cormac gets in aboot the fine Scottish Whisky's that JJ keeps putting down in front of him to keep him happy. Alberto put on a lovely lunch for them all and when everything is settled down, JJ stands up to address the family.

"Ladies and Gents, myself, my Mum and Teresa are all so happy that yous are here. I know the past few months have been a bit of a whirlwind with James dying, Teresa getting pregnant, the Wedding and the family finding out about Father Peter Jackson. He's buried not too far from here so I thought it'd be nice to take yous to meet him. Cormac, Mairead and Karen, do you want to meet your big brother?".

Now this could go either way here. The big yin has had a few whiskys now and he's got hawns like shovels. If he reaches out and cracks me one then there'll be no wedding on Saturday.

"Of course we do my boy, let's go!!" shouts Cormac.

JJ breathes a huge sigh of relief and takes the Healy's out of the pub, along Main Street and up Sweets Way and then in to the Cemetery. He leads them all to Father Peter Jackson's grave.

"Well, Cormac, Mairead and Karen, this is where your big brother Peter rests. I know that Teresa has told you all about "The Bunnet" now and this is where this all started. I got "The Bunnet" from the Father's boxes in the Charity shop here and it was your James that led me to it".

"This is exactly where I proposed to Teresa as well once I broke the news to her that Peter was actually her biological Uncle. Peter was a great man and I knew him all my life. I was one of his Alter Boys and his stories were legendary. Trust me when I say this, he had an amazing life".

"The Bunnet JJ?" asks Terry.

"I'll explain it all in a minute Mum" says JJ. "Let's go for a walk and I'll tell you all about it and we'll leave Teresa's family here with Peter".

JJ leave's the Healy's to speak with Peter and look at his grave. He takes his Mum a walk around the Cemetery. He tells her everything about how he met James to ending up with the Bunnet. He explains everything about his trip to Ireland, the letter he got from James and how he ended up owning the Textiles Factory before giving it to her. It all starts to make sense to Terry now and she can't believe it all really.

"So "The Bunnet" is gone for good then JJ?" says Terry.

"Yes Mum it has but look at what it's done for all of our lives" says JJ. "If it wasn't for "The Bunnet" then so much wouldn't have happened. The Pub and the Factory would be flats now owned by Longshanks and you wouldn't be an upcoming Granny and Mother in Law either".

"True son, true" says Terry.

Teresa walks over to them both whilst the rest of the Healy's are still paying their respects to Father Jackson's grave.

"JJ, that was lovely what you said up there it really was. I'm just glad we can all put "The Bunnet" thing to rest now as well. I'm sorry that we never told you about it Terry but probably today was the right time".

"No yer fine Teresa, it looks like no harm was done with it and JJ never got greedy with it thankfully. It's brought us all together if anything, so I'm glad that James passed it on to him".

The family all say their goodbyes to Father Peter Jackson for now and head back to Healy's. As they walk in Tina starts shouting at them to come in quickly. The National News is about to start and the sentencing is in.

"We can cross live to our Crime Correspondent Niall Paterson who is at the High Court in Glasgow for us today for the sentencing of Serial Killer Peter Black and his old boss Mr Longshanks. What can you tell us Niall?".

"Well Kay, what I can tell you is that for the triple murder of Mel, Marie and Bonnie in that sleepy West Coast of Scotland Town, Peter Black will do life without the chance of parole".

"What about Mr Longshanks Niall?"

"Well, his lawyers wanted to take into consideration his age. At 72 years old, they tried to get him a lighter sentence but the judge was having none of it. He told Mr Longshanks that he was one of the most despicable characters that he'd ever came across and for "Conspiracy to Murder" Longshanks was sentenced to life in Prison as well with a minimum of 25 years".

"A good result all round then Niall?"

"Yes Kay, both men will now die in Glasgow's notorious Barlinnie Prison".

"Ya fucking dancer!!" shouts JJ.

CHAPTER TWENTY FIVE

THE BIG DAY ARRIVES

The town is buzzing with the recent news about Pedro Black and Mr Longshanks getting sent down the other day and finally the big day has arrived for JJ & Teresa. JJ stayed at Hugo's last night and Teresa is with all the girls at Rose's getting their hair done.

Russell from Phoenix Taxi's has provided all the Luxury Cars today for free as his gift to the couple. A fancy Jaguar for the boys to arrive in and the ladies get a Rolls Royce. Cormac is going to give Teresa away as her Dad died many years ago and her Aunty Karen is her Maid of Honour. Her cousins Frances and Margaret are her Bridesmaids.

"Holy fucking shitballs Hugo, I'm bricking it man" says JJ.

"Och calm doon man, ye'll be fine. Remember the good auld days in the bookies when oor horse and another horse were neck and neck reaching for the line. Noo that was bricking it boy".

"Well it's worse than that Hugo. If I could shit bricks the noo, I could build ten hotels".

The whole town is buzzing for the wedding and Rose's shop is mobbed. The Factory Girls were in from 7.30am and everybody has been given slots. The wedding party arrives at 10am with the wedding at 2pm.

"Hiya lassies" says Rose.

"Hi Rose" says all.

Teresa introduces all the ladies from the Healy clan to Rose and she and her little helpers get started on the wedding party. The Factory Girls are all meeting at Donna's at 12 o'clock for a couple of drinks before heading to the Chapel for the wedding at 2pm.

"Aw lassies, ye's all look gorgeous the day with all yer hair done and yer nice dresses on" says Donna.

"I canny wait for this the day, they're such a lovely couple" says Lisa.

"Aye, I hope Teresa has got comfy trainers on under that dress cause she's getting huge now" says Debbie.

"Aye the poor thing" says Babs. "I hope they don't have her standing too long today".

"I'm looking forward to Siham's the night, we had a right ball in there last Saturday" says Clare.

"Aye the place is absolutely beautiful inside. It's gonna be some day and night that's for sure" says Kirsty.

"I feel like this is an end of an era today lassies" says Jan. "Efter today, the town is just going to go back to normal isn't it? It's been mental recently and such a rollercoaster".

"It has Jan aye but we can be proud of our wee toon and more importantly, proud of ourselves lassies" says Donna.

"Here here".

Simon has made it back for the wedding and he's round at his Mum Tina's house getting ready.

"So who's this big date you've got today son?".

"Och it's no big date Mum, I'm just taking a pal".

"Aye aye" says Tina.

It's 1.30pm and everybody starts to arrive at the Chapel. At 1.40pm this flash Jaguar stops outside the Chapel and out gets Hugo and JJ. There's a round of applause from everybody as they make their way inside with all the guests. Hugo and JJ make their way up to the altar and greet the Priest.

"How you doing Father?" says JJ.

"Fine son, and you?"

"I don't want to swear in the Chapel haha".

2.10pm and the Organist starts blaring out "Here Comes the Bride".

JJ turns round to see his beautiful bride being led down the aisle by her Uncle Cormac. He can hardly believe his eyes at her beauty. She's eight months pregnant and beats any supermodel out there. Perfection!! Everybody looks amazing and the Priest gives a beautiful wedding service.

They leave the Chapel to a massive round of applause as Husband and Wife. Confetti and rice is everywhere as the couple navigate their way to the awaiting Rolls Royce and get in.

"I love you Jamie Johnson" says Teresa.

"And I love you Teresa Johnson" says JJ.

They share a passionate kiss and the driver takes them a drive around the seaside town to give the guests time to get to Siham's first to greet them at the reception.

As they pull up to Siham's, everybody is there. Hugo with the bridesmaids and all the Healy's. The Factory girls are all there as are all the punters from the pub. Simon is with his date Rose the Hairdresser and even Sammy from the shops is there in his best suit.

They all head into Siham's and the wedding party get to the top table and everybody else takes their seats. Once the perfectly cooked five course dinner is served up by Alberto and his team and devoured, Hugo stands up to deliver his Best Man's speech. The room goes quiet.

"Ladies and Gentlemen, I've known this wee guy all of his life. He's always been a wee bugger so he has. Even the day, I canny get away from the wee shite. When he was a wee boy and he'd be walking down Main Street hand in hand with his wee maw Terry, I gave him a pound note wan day, he must've been about four. Little did I know that he was going to shout me and stop me every single time I seen him, and every single time after that for one".

"So JJ, you owe me about Four Grand mate".

"No, like I said, I've known him since he was a wee boy, he's like a son to me".

"Awwwwwwww" is the sound from the crowd.

"He was like a mini me and we had some good times in the bookies and we also had some bad times but who'd have thought that two mad gamblers who did nothing but sit in a bookies all day would end up with two very special establishments eh?".

"I'm proud of what he's came from to what he is today. He's got himself a beautiful wife from Ireland from a beautiful family and if they raise their child the way JJ's wee maw raised him, then they have a beautiful human being on their hands. I love you JJ pal, you're one special boy son".

"I'd like evryone to stand and join in me in toasting, the Bride and Groom!!"

"The Bride and Groom!!" says all.

There's a big round of applause and not a dry eye in the house.

"Lovely speech Hugo mate" says JJ, as Hugo takes his seat.

"I meant every word wee man".

The rest of the speeches get done and the party gets started. Everybody is having a ball barring Teresa.

"Mum, can you unloosen me dress a bit please? I can hardly breath in this".

Mairead and Terry take Teresa into the toilet to unloosen her wedding dress a bit.

Rose is with Simon at the Bar.

"Do you have to go back to Spain Simon?".

"I do Rose aye".

"Jist stay here wi me pal. I'll look efter ye".

"It's tempting Rose it really is but it's a no. I don't belong here anymore, it's changed so much and I'm at home over there now".

"Oh ok pal, well, you know I'll always be here for you".

"I know pal, I know".

There's a loud scream from the ladies toilet. The DJ "Jimmy" stops the music.

"JJ quick quick, come to the Ladies toilets shouts Terry".

JJ rushes to the ladies toilets and Teresa is sat on the floor in a pool of water with her mum Mairead holding her hand. Today of all days, Teresa's waters have broken. The baby is on it's way!!

CHAPTER TWENTY SIX

THE PERFECT ENDING

The ambulance is phoned right away and it's at Siham's within five minutes. JJ instructs Hugo to address the crowd and let them know that the night still goes ahead. JJ gets into the ambulance with Teresa, and Russell is called to take the rest of the family in a minibus to follow the ambulance to the hospital.

"I'm scared JJ" says Teresa.

"Don't be darling" says JJ. "You're in the best hands now and everything is gonna be alright baby".

They get to the hospital within twenty minutes and Teresa is taken straight into the Labour Room where they quickly wire her up and start taking some tests. The Healy's are all outside with Terry and they're all worried sick. JJ is inside with Teresa.

"The Midwife said everything is fine darling, you just try and relax" says JJ.

"Try and fecking relax Jamie Johnson, have you ever had a contraction?".

Teresa is screaming with the pain and her poor family can here the screams outside. It's a tense few hours and JJ keeps swapping with Mairead so that she can be with her daughter at her time of need as well. The Midwife will only let one person in at a time.

Mairead is stroking Teresa's hair and trying to calm her down. She has some news for her, and whilst they're away from the rest of the family, she decides to break it to her.

"Terry phoned me darling and told me all about your worries and fears. I've bought a wee apartment down the shore front next to Siham's and all my stuff arrives in the morning darling". "I'm moving here to be closer to you and the babby Teresa".

"Awwwww Mammy" says Teresa.

They both burst out crying and they embrace. The Midwife informs Mairead that she better get JJ in as they are about to start pushing.

"JJ, you've to go in son" she's going to start pushing" says Mairead.

Terry gives JJ a hug.

"This is the moment your life is about to change son" says Terry.

JJ goes inside and poor Teresa is chalk white and covered in sweat. He takes the cloth and the bowl of water and starts dabbing her forehead and face to cool her down.

"You can do this baby" says JJ as he grabs her hand.

"Are you ready now Mrs Johnson?" says the Midwife. "OK, just like we said now, PUSH!!".

For two hours, she's pushing and trying with all of her might to get the baby out. There's talk of a C-Section when finally the baby comes out.

"It's a boy Mr and Mrs Johnson, a Baby Boy!!" says the midwife.

JJ kisses Teresa and wipes her down with the cool cloth. They're both crying their eyes out and the midwife lays the wee boy on Teresa's bare chest.

"Oh JJ, he's absolutely gorgeous. Run out and tell everyone".

JJ runs outside to the corridor.

"It's a BOY everybody!!"

He runs down the corridor and big Cormac grabs him first. JJ nearly passes out with the bear hug. The Midwife comes out to speak to the family.

"Everything has went perfectly folks. He's four weeks early but he's a healthy 6lbs 2oz's. Once we've cleaned up the room and Mrs Johnson, yous are all more than welcome to come in and meet the new arrival".

Mairead and Terry are hugging each other and crying their eyes out. Aiden high fives JJ and the whole contingent are just on top of the world. JJ messages Hugo to let him know. Fifteen minutes go by and the Midwife signals the family into the room to see the new arrival.

Meanwhile back at the wedding reception Hugo goes up to speak to Jimmy and asks to be able to address the crowd when the next song finishes.

"That was Come on Eileen folks, I hope you enjoyed that wee blast from the past cause I know I did" says Jimmy. "The Best Man Hugo has a few words he'd like to say to everyone".

"Cheers Jimmy!! Right folks, I have some good news from the hospital. Teresa has had her baby and I've to let you all know that it's a healthy 6lbs 2oz baby boy that they've had".

Everybody starts cheering and clapping.

"Now", says Hugo. "JJ assures me he's going to give me this back so there's £1000 behind the bar as well now to help you all the celebrate the birth of his baby boy".

Before Hugo could even finish his sentence, Jan was at the front of the queue all ready to get the drinks in for the Factory Girls.

Back at the hospital, the family are in to see the new baby boy and they're discussing names.

"I think Cormac is a belter of a name my boy" Cormac says to JJ.

"You're right Cormac it is but we've came up with a name haven't we Teresa?" says JJ.

"We have indeed darling" says Teresa.

"This whole story started with one man and one man only really and that was Father Peter Jackson" said JJ. "If it wasn't for him really, then none of us would be standing here today. We thought about naming him Peter but since the recent Serial Killer in the town was called Peter, we decided against that.

"Jackson as well was probably a bit much, so we've decided to shorten it a wee bit and go with Jax. We both think it's a cool name so everybody, say hello to Jax Johnson".

"Another JJ? says Terry.

"Oh shoite, I never taught of that now sure" says Teresa. "Can we change it JJ haha?".

Teresa is soon to be moved up to the ward and the Midwife says that she'll be free to leave in the morning. The family say their goodbyes and head back to catch the last hour of the reception.

"Go with them JJ" says Teresa. "I need my rest darling. Come back and get me in the morning sure".

"Are you sure baby?" says JJ.

"Go man go" she said.

JJ gives Teresa a kiss and heads out to jump in a taxi back to Siham's for the last wee hour. He walks in to an almighty roar and everybody is congratulating him. After half an hour or so once everybody leaves him alone, his Mum walks up to him.

"JJ, myself and the Factory Girls would like to chat to you alone on the roof terrace please because it's far too bloody noisy in here".

"No bother Mum, I'll be up the noo".

JJ walks up the stairs to the roof and there's eight ladies waiting for him on the roof. He closes the door behind him to drown out the sound of the music from downstairs.

"Christ, I feel intimidated here haha" says JJ. "Ye's are no gonna fling me aff the roof are ye's?".

"No no son" says Terry. "I was telling the lassies the story about how you and Teresa met and stuff and they have a wee gift for you. Well no for you but for wee Jax".

"Oh ok" says JJ.

Donna, Kirsty, Jan, Clare, Debbie, Lisa and Babs are all standing a semi circle all looking as proud as punch and Donna has a tiny wee cardboard box in her hand.

"JJ, yer maw telt us the story and we've lived a part of it with you son, it's been an emotional rollercoaster of a journey and with that, we got this gift for wee Jax to wear with pride".

JJ takes the box from Donna and opens it. It's a wee Brown Bunnet with a Four Leaf Clover stitched on the side of it.

THE END

The story "The Factory Girls" was by Scott Alcroft.

I'd like to dedicate this book to two very special people in my life. So special in fact that I ended up putting them in this book.

First up is a guy named Russell Drummond. Russell has been there for me on countless times when I've needed him in the past. Russell is a guy that I depended on and to have a person like that in my life, last year especially, when I needed people the most, was priceless. I hope you have a healthy future Russell and thank you for everything. Phoenix Taxi's in Irvine that are actually featured in the book is Russell's company so if you ever need a taxi folks.

The second person is a lady named Rose Price. Again, Rose is a Hairdresser and is featured in the book. Rose, like Russell, was a great person for me as my marriage was breaking down. I was at the saddest point in my life and she did nothing but cheer me up on a daily basis. She was a massive part of my final few years in Scotland and again, this is my way of saying thank you.

Printed in Poland
by Amazon Fulfillment
Poland Sp. z o.o., Wrocław